Giraffe of
Montana

VOLUME I

Written By

William Bowman Piper

Little Pemberley Press
Houston, TX
2005

Little Pemberley Press
1528 Tulane Street, Suite F
Houston, TX 77008
713-862-8542

www.littlepemberleypress.com

Second Printing 2010

10-Digit ISBN# 0-9763359-4-8
13-Digit ISBN# 978-0-9763359-4-8

Piper, William Bowman, 1927-
    Giraffe of Montana / by William Bowman Piper.
    p. cm. — (Giraffe of Montana ; v. 1)
    SUMMARY: A giraffe living in Montana and his animal
friends share adventures and the ups and downs of daily life.
    Audience: Ages 6-10.
    ISBN 0-9763359-4-8 ; 978-0-9763359-4-8
    1. Animals—Juvenile fiction. [1. Animals—Fiction.
    2. Friendship—Fiction. 3. Montana—Fiction.] I. Title.
    PZ10.3.P412Gir 2005   [E] QBI05-600033

Book Production Team
Consulting & Coordination — Rita Mills of The Book Connection
Editing — Faye Walker

Cover Design & Illustration — Bill Megenhardt

The paper used in this publication meets the requirements of the American National Stan-
dard for Permanence of Paper for Printed Library Materials Z39.48-1984.
Printed in the United States of America

for Isabel

Acknowledgements

The author wishes to thank
Rita Mills, the compositor and publishing consultant,
Bill Megenhardt, the illustrator and cover designer,
and Faye Walker, the editor.
This book has become almost as much theirs as his.

Table of Contents

Friends

❄ ❄ ❄

Giraffe made his home in a comfortable cave in the middle of Montana. Although he lived by himself and was indeed the only one of his kind in the whole state, he was never lonely.

The path that ran west from his cave led beneath the tree in which Peter o'Possum lived with his family and skirted the mound in which Kanga and Roo, except when they were visiting England, made their home. About a mile further on, it led to the royal palace where the king and queen of Montana lived with their two daughters, Princess Isabel and Isabel, and with their two servants, Oscar the footman and Catherine the cook. (Be sure, by the way, not to confuse Oscar the footman with Dr. Oscar the orangutan.) The path that ran north led in a few yards to the pond of Hal the hippo and Casper the crocodile. Needless to say, all these folks were friends of Giraffe.

The stream, which flowed, as Rudolph the raccoon informed Giraffe, from the pond all the way to the Pacific Ocean, led to still other friends. Rudolph himself burrowed in a bank of this stream. And in the woods beyond lived the beavers, who cut down a few trees at bankside to construct the dams in which they raised their families. Giraffe's special friends among the beavers were Billy and his cousin, Bo Bo. Bo Bo had less fat in his tail than a beaver should have, as he was painfully aware, but Giraffe knew him to be a generous and amiable beaver for all that. Billy, as everyone knew, had designed and built the Montana railroad and served also as its engineer.

The path that ran south from Giraffe's cave sloped down to the creek, which, as Rudolph explained to Giraffe, flowed east until it reached "the father of waters;" then it sloped up into the meadow where Giraffe could almost always find the zebras, Zane and Zack, Ella the elephant, and

Leo the lion, and sometimes stumble across Marvin the mole, although Marvin was likely to pop up almost any place.

The northern path, after it skirted the pond, plunged through evergreen woods and ended, after a hike, at the home of Gloria the gorilla. Gloria had been able to raise the only banana trees ever to grow in Montana. Some way to the east—although not quite to "the father of waters"—Giraffe and his friends could find Dr. Oscar the orangutan whenever they took sick or were hurt in an accident. Everybody remembered the time—how could they forget?—when Billy the beaver's tail got trapped under a log, and Marvin the mole freed him: the bandage Dr. Oscar had put on Billy's tail Giraffe and his friends discussed with admiration long after Billy's tail was healed.

So you can see, Giraffe was surrounded by friends. And although he was the special friend of Princess Isabel, all the residents of Montana loved him; and none of them, not even Peter o'Possum, were jealous: after all, she was a princess. What is probably more important, Giraffe loved all of them.

It should be easy to understand, then, why he was concerned when he was having a dip in the pond one day and Casper the crocodile swam silently up behind him and, after clearing his throat, broke into great crocodile tears, real tears, mind you, that dribbled out of Casper's eyes and plopped into the pond right where Giraffe was standing up to his knees in the chilly water.

"What's wrong, Casper?" Giraffe asked in some alarm.

He had always believed his friend was as happy in Montana and as well adjusted as he was himself. Surely the pond was a pleasant home, well-stocked with the kind of fish Casper relished; and although it froze over in the rugged Montana winters, Casper could just stiffen and sleep if he wanted to and then wake up supple and hungry in the spring. Hal the hippo, moreover, who shared the pond with him through all the warm months of the year, was a very good friend, quite attentive and companionable; and there wasn't any trouble about food because Hal ate only green slime, and there was plenty of that on the floor of the pond. So what could be wrong?

"I'm lonely, Giraffe," Casper said, gulping back his tears, "I'm so lonely!"

Giraffe knew what loneliness was well enough. There had been a time, not many months before, when Princess Isabel, who was feeling a little neglected herself at the time, had begun to worry about him living all alone in his cave—but that's another story.

When Casper complained about being lonely, at any rate, Giraffe understood what he was feeling. But what could he do? Nothing. Or, at least, nothing occurred to him—not at first. But Giraffe was a thoughtful friend, and as he turned Casper's unhappiness over in his mind in the next few days, he remembered a report Hal the hippo had brought back from Florida last spring. Hal had visited relatives in the zoo down there, traveling in the car Billy the beaver had designed and made just for him and had attached to the Florida train for his trip. Billy the beaver, who was very accommodating to his friends, had made an especially ingenious adjustment to Giraffe's car for the trip he took with Princess Isabel to Billings to see *The Wizard of Oz*—but that is also another story.

Hal had returned to Montana from his visit to the Florida Zoo with a lot of news—one item, for example, about Giraffe's little niece, Eugenia the giraffe, getting her foot caught in a bucket, which turned out to be a very funny item indeed. But Hal had also brought back a story, which wasn't so funny, about Allison the albino alligator. It seems, as Hal understood the situation, Allison was not at all self-conscious about her color—why should she be? She would have been happy to bask all day beside the little pool before the great glass window Mr. Masters the manager had provided for her and let all the children who visited the reptile house admire her full twelve feet of glistening white scales— if she had not felt so shy about her snub nose. It is true, her nose was very snubbed indeed, especially in comparison to the Roman noses displayed by every one of the family of crocodiles, who lived in the glass house right next to hers.

"They never let me forget," she complained to her attendant: "Look how they lift up their heads and yawn, even the babies, just to show off their fine long noses."

The attendant was only too ready to report this to the keepers of the snakes and the lizards with whom he shared his lunch: some people are so thoughtless. Soon it was known throughout the zoo, even as far away as the hippo pen, Allison was ashamed of her nose. This was why she hid behind the cypress log in her home from the time the zoo opened in the morning until the time it closed at night.

This made Mr. Masters the manager pretty mad, as you may imagine. Visitors, especially those who brought their children, kept asking him about the famous albino alligator. They had waited and waited beside the case in which she was supposed to be kept—but no alligator; just a big old cypress log beside an empty pool. They didn't believe the zoo had such an alligator at all. When they said this sort of thing, Mr. Masters would stamp from foot to foot in a way he had when he was upset.

He spoke to Allison at some length, bobbing his head up and down in another way he had, about what he called her lack of cooperation. You see, he didn't understand Allison's feelings. He was not a cruel person, but he did not have as much sympathy for his reptiles as he should have had: monkeys were his special pets, and I'm afraid he was inclined to play favorites. But he did try to encourage Allison, and although she couldn't bear to tell him about her snub nose— "after all," as she later explained to Giraffe, "he could hardly fail to notice it"—she promised to show herself to the children at least to some extent. The next day, the kids who passed by the "Albino Alligator" case saw two or three feet of shapely white scales sticking out from behind the cypress log and waving in what Allison hoped was a friendly way.

Mr. Masters was furious when Allison's attendant reported this: "I provide that reptile a nice big pen," he said, stamping from foot to foot: "I have the water in her pool changed every day, I see she gets plenty of fish—not to speak of her vitamin supplement, and all I want is for her to bask part of the day in front of the big glass window so the children can see her. Is this," he asked, bobbing his head up and down, "so unreasonable?"

But two or three feet of her tail was all Allison was able to show.

That was how matters stood, with Mr. Masters threatening to drive Allison from her home, when Hal returned to Montana. At first Giraffe merely sympathized with Allison and agreed with Hal to hope for the best. But before long, Casper's loneliness occurred to him, and he saw or thought he saw how rescuing Allison from the zoo—if he could do it—might also provide a cure for Casper. His friend really was a melancholy spectacle these days basking all alone beneath the pale Montana sun.

❄ ❄ ❄

With this in mind, Giraffe paid a visit to the pond, and, as luck would have it, he found both Casper and Hal there discussing the problem of the community Christmas tree, a matter I will get to by-and-by.

"Well, Casper," Giraffe said, in what he hoped would be a jovial tone, "I'm glad to find you in the Christmas spirit."

"I'm trying," said Casper. "I don't want to ruin things for all our friends."

"But he's feeling a little blue, let me tell you," said Hal, who knew Casper well and was quite worried about him.

"Blue?" said Giraffe, who had been thinking of Allison.

"Sad," Hal responded, "I mean sad."

"Oh!" said Giraffe, "oh, yes. But Christmas is such a cheery time. I bet you enjoy it, Casper, especially when Princess Isabel and Isabel and all our friends gather together around the tree."

He was about to begin asking them what ideas they had about the tree when he remembered he had come down to the pond with something else in mind. But he wasn't sure how to bring it up.

Just then Hal ducked his head into the water where he was standing, plowed into a bunch of slime, and came back up with a delicious mouthful, which he chomped with obvious pleasure. He had scooped up so much that knots and threads of green hung down all around his jaw. Suddenly Giraffe knew what to say.

"You're lucky to have such a fine snub nose, Hal," he remarked with admiration: "It really helps you scrape the bottom of the pond."

"Yes," Hal replied with satisfaction, "I can make a full meal, let me tell you, in just two or three scoops."

"And I must say," Giraffe added, "it's a very handsome nose as well."

"Thank you, Giraffe," Hal responded grandly: "I've always considered myself a good-looking hippo."

"You're certainly the best-looking one in Montana,"

said Giraffe. And the two friends laughed heartily at Giraffe's joke. Even Casper smiled a little.

"Of course," Casper said, interrupting his friends in their amusement, "I've always held a long slender nose is the best and handsomest and surely the most elegant." Then he raised his head and yawned so his two friends could see what he meant.

"I suppose," Giraffe suggested, "you would always feel personally superior to someone with a snub nose—a nose like Hal's."

"Why, no," Casper said, snapping his jaws. "I can surely take pride in my own appearance, and yet accept other kinds of looks as well."

"*Accept,*" answered Giraffe, "but you couldn't become close to a person with such a nose, I mean, really close to someone with a really snubbed nose?"

"Like Hal, you mean?" Casper responded.

"Yes," Giraffe said, "but with someone perhaps somewhat like you in other ways. You wouldn't want to bask all day in the sun with such a companion."

"Well," said Casper, smiling with a broad crocodile smile, "maybe not with Hal: he would take up too much of my little patio."

"I'm not planning to join you up there, let me tell you," Hal assured his scaly friend: "Wallowing in the pond here is more my thing." But then Hal, who suddenly remembered Allison the alligator and began to see what Giraffe was driving at, added with some solemnity, "I might like to bask along side you one of these days—one of these cool Montana mornings if it was a little overcast, of course—I can't take too much of the sun, let me tell you—that is, if you wouldn't be embarrassed to share your beach with such a snub nose."

"Certainly not," Casper replied: "I'd welcome you with a nice fish salad, and we'd have a picnic."

"Hal may take you up on that before long," Giraffe said with a smile, "and if not Hal, someone with just as much of a snub nose, someone who might like to share your fish salad."

"Not you, Giraffe," Casper said, "you'll have to visit Peter o'Possum if you want salad made from tender little tree leaves." And the three friends had another good laugh: the idea of Casper the crocodile scrambling up the trunk of an elm or oak to fetch a leaf salad for Giraffe was pretty funny.

Casper didn't know why, but this conversation made him feel better than he had for a long time.

Hal and Giraffe exchanged a glance as Giraffe turned to go down the path to his cave: they both realized that Giraffe was soon going to pay a visit to his relatives in the Florida Zoo.

Billy the beaver was happy to attach Giraffe's special car to the Florida train when Giraffe announced his plans to visit his relatives. Giraffe decided not to mention his other plans until he had actually carried them out. When

Billy told Bo Bo about Giraffe's trip, Bo Bo immediately started gathering bark. And when he had a sack full, he took it up to the palace where Catherine the cook, under instructions from Princess Isabel, turned it into a pail of savory bark broth, spiced just the way Catherine knew Giraffe liked it. When Peter o'Possum learned about Giraffe's trip, he and all the little possums began scampering up the trees, the oaks, birches, maples, sycamores, and elms, which grew near the great pine tree they themselves inhabited, to collect a basket of tender leaves—enough to nourish Giraffe during his whole journey to Florida and back: that had to be a pretty big basket.

On the day of Giraffe's departure, many of his friends assembled at the station. Princess Isabel and Isabel walked over from the palace followed by Oscar the footman, carrying the pail of bark broth; Zane and Zack bore two baskets of leaves the possums had gathered. Kanga and Roo brought a jar of honey from their own stock, and Gloria the gorilla arrived with a stalk of bananas. They loaded all these good things into Giraffe's car. The leaves were dumped carefully into the manger Billy the beaver had fastened to the far end of the car; and the pail of broth was hooked to a big nail Billy had driven into the wall right beside it. The bananas were hung from the roof to keep them fresh in case Giraffe wanted one; the jar of honey Billy stored in a safe place in the caboose.

"Oh," said Kanga, when she savored the broth: "Doesn't it smell good, Roo?" She was always trying to get Roo to eat what she called "more nourishing food."

This praise of Princess Isabel's gift annoyed Peter o'Possum a little bit, and he said, somewhat severely, "I furnished all the tender leaves Zane and Zack are carrying onto Giraffe's car."

"Yes," said Isabel, who understood Peter's feelings, "and I see you collected all different kinds to provide our friend some variety: there are oak leaves and elm and birch."

"Yes," said Peter, "and we found some sycamore and maple leaves, too—and they are not so easy to come by."

"It is surely a nice treat for Giraffe," Isabel agreed.

Bo Bo the beaver, who overheard this conversation, was inclined to tell how he and other beavers had gathered the bark for Giraffe's broth, but he decided not to: he was a very thoughtful beaver despite his having too little fat in his tail.

Princess Isabel, however, couldn't help boasting a little about how she had helped Catherine prepare the broth. "The spice," she said, "is a special palace secret."

"Well," said Billy the beaver, as he lowered the gangplank so Giraffe could climb aboard, "you have all worked together to make our friend's travel comfortable." Everybody seemed to be satisfied with that.

Casper, who had bid Giraffe goodbye the night before down by the pond, didn't attend: it was a little too far to the station for him to walk. But Hal waddled over, huffing and puffing.

"I'm much more agile on land, let me tell you, than you might expect," he told Leo the lion, whom he ran into along the way.

Leo, who had a scarlet bow woven by his wife, Lucy, into the tuft of his tail to honor the occasion, merely strutted on. Rudolph the raccoon showed up perched on the back of Ella the elephant who was wearing a big red sign, "Hurry home, Giraffe." Since it was still several weeks before Christmas, Rudolf the red-nosed reindeer (not to be confused with Rudolph the raccoon) was also able to come by to bid his friend Giraffe farewell. And even Marvin the mole popped up in time to wave at the train. It was a very festive departure.

As Giraffe mounted the gang plank, Rudolph the raccoon shouted after him, "Be sure to visit the home of Henry Clay as you pass through Lexington—and Mary Todd Lincoln's home, too, if you have enough time."

After the train left Montana, Giraffe settled down in the car Billy the beaver had prepared for him. Bo Bo the beaver had realized that his tail, despite its deficiency, made an excellent brush; and he had used it to paint the walls of the car so it resembled the inside of Giraffe's cave to help him feel at home on long trips. Billy the beaver had cut a skylight in the roof so Giraffe could stretch his neck as the train rolled along and take in the sights. They considered laying wall-to-wall moss on the floor, but decided to settle for a nice litter of straw. All in all, Giraffe traveled in great comfort.

The train passed through Lexington at night, only whistling at the crossing as it rolled on, but the day before, Giraffe did have a chance to stretch his neck out of his skylight and take in "the father of waters." He made a mental note to tell Rudolph the raccoon about it when he got back to Montana. Otherwise, because Billy was a good engineer, the trip was uneventful. And that was just as well, because, as you may understand, Giraffe had a lot on his mind.

❄ ❄ ❄

When Billy the beaver unloaded him at the Florida Zoo, Giraffe went right to the giraffe yard to see his relatives. He was especially eager to visit with his niece, Eugenia the giraffe, and make sure she hadn't suffered any bad after-effects from that bucket. Her foot, which she displayed with pride, had just about healed, and although her mother, Ginny the giraffe, remembered the whole affair with horror—that's how mothers are—Eugenia felt pretty pleased at all the commotion she had caused: "Mr. Masters the manager came by just to see how I was. He brought me a banana." After enjoying a brief visit with Ginny and sharing a nice platter of selected leaves—very tasty—with all his relatives, Giraffe strolled over to the main office of the zoo to see Mr. Masters the manager.

He had to duck his head to get into Mr. Masters's office, and he had to tuck his legs under him to seat himself on the carpet in front of Mr. Master's fine oak desk. But he managed it more gracefully than you might imagine. Almost as soon as he was settled, he began, "I understand there is an unhappy and uncooperative alligator living here at the zoo." He was anxious about Mr. Masters's response and feared the manager might resist any assault on the population of his domain.

"Yes," said Mr. Masters, as he reached his hand across his chest to scratch his armpit, "Allison the alligator has proven to be both impolite and undutiful—despite several long talks I have had with her." After giving himself a good scratch, he went on: "I wish she'd act more like the monkeys, or like the seals, for that matter. Have you visited the seals' tank, Giraffe, especially at feeding time? They put on quite a show! I don't expect Allison to be so lively as the seals, of course; but she could come out from behind her old cypress log now and then to bask in front of the glass so the children—and their parents—will at least believe the Florida Zoo has an alligator.

"Don't you agree, Giraffe?" Mr. Masters the manager asked, bobbing his head up and down. "She really ought to yawn occasionally and show off her nose, so visitors to the zoo can see the difference between alligators and crocodiles. Waving a little bit of her tail, Giraffe, this is just not enough." He came out from behind his desk, he was so upset, and began stamping from foot to foot.

"I've been told," Giraffe replied, "Allison is ashamed of her nose; and showing it off, especially in contrast with the Roman noses next door, might be humiliating."

"Yes," agreed Mr. Masters, bobbing his head up and down again, "but she is an alligator after all."

"True," said Giraffe, "but she's a person, too—and a person, apparently, who has very delicate feelings."

"Well," Mr. Masters replied with a sigh, reaching

his hand up and bending his wrist so he could scratch the top of his head, "what do you suggest, Giraffe?"

"That is a question," Giraffe admitted, putting as much sympathy into his voice as he could.

While he was sympathizing with Mr. Masters the manager, however, Giraffe thought to himself, "This isn't going to be as hard as I feared."

"Actually," Mr. Masters said with some dignity, "I've just about reached an agreement with a whole family of gators to live here if I can find someplace else for Allison. They are a sociable family, too, I assure you, Giraffe. One or another of them will be on display every minute the zoo is open: they've agreed to that." And he bobbed his head up and down with satisfaction.

"Well," said Giraffe in his most amiable tone, "it seems, Mr. Masters, you have something of a problem. You can't just put Allison out on the street: that would create quite a commotion—a lot more than my niece Eugenia's getting her foot caught in the bucket!"

"True, true," said Mr. Masters the manager, scratching the top of his head again. "What can we do?"

"What indeed?" Giraffe mused, as if trying to come up with something. Then, after a pause, he said, "There is a nice pond near my home in Montana, a pond well stocked with fish, in which a single reptile, Casper the crocodile, has resided for the last few years."

"Montana?" Mr. Masters echoed with some surprise. "It's awfully cold up there, isn't it?—And far away," he said, bobbing his head up and down.

"Casper," Giraffe answered, "has adjusted very well to Montana: he sleeps through the winter in a cozy mud burrow, which he's in the process of enlarging, by the way; and then, when spring comes, he and the pond thaw at just about the same time; he stretches, blinks, and begins fishing again."

"Doesn't he get stiff in the winter?" asked Mr. Masters.

"Yes, but he limbers up nicely when the weather warms, and he's very hungry, as you may imagine. Of course," Giraffe continued, "we must be sure Allison would adjust happily to such a situation. Casper basks on the bank of the pond closest to my cave, which is, indeed, just a few steps away; and I'm sure he would welcome her company. The only other inhabitant of the pond itself is Hal the hippo, and although he and Casper are on excellent terms, Hal is hardly a suitable basking companion."

"No," said Mr. Masters, reaching up again to scratch his armpit, "I would think not." He and Giraffe shared a little laugh.

"It is hard," Giraffe admitted, "to imagine Hal, who is quite a big hippo, basking beside his slender, elegant friend. Allison, on the other hand—"

"But what about Allison's snub nose?" Mr. Masters asked, bobbing his head up and down: "Might not Casper find fault with that? The crocs who live right beside her here in the zoo are quite superior. How would Allison respond—she's so sensitive?" While thinking this over, Mr. Masters the manager started again to stamp slowly from one of his feet to the other.

"A good question, Mr. Masters," said Giraffe, bowing his head, "but, as it happens, I've had a serious talk with Casper about this very thing, and I've become convinced he'd be so happy to have a basking companion, one who could share a fish lunch with him—Hal the hippo is, of course, vegetarian—he would hardly notice Allison's nose at all. She is, otherwise, a lovely creature, I understand, with a long white scaly figure: I believe Casper would find her quite acceptable. You know, Mr. Masters," Giraffe suggested, gazing with sincerity at Mr. Masters's flat dish-shaped countenance, "a snub nose can be becoming and, not only that, but appropriate as well." Then Giraffe told Mr. Masters about the conversation he'd had with Casper and Hal beside the pond in Montana.

"Yes," said Mr. Masters, bobbing his head up and down, "but Montana is so far away. And alligator travel, even for short distances, presents lots of difficulties. I'm afraid, Giraffe, we'll have to find some other solution to the Allison problem."

This made Giraffe very happy, and he replied, "I'm glad you have brought that up, Mr. Masters, because the same thing has been bothering me. But when I mentioned it to Billy the beaver, who is the engineer of the Montana railroad, he became very interested. Has he ever shown you the splendid train car he and his cousin, Bo Bo the beaver, have created for me?" *Created* was, as Giraffe knew, a very grand word to describe the modifications the beavers had made in his car, but he needed to get Mr. Masters's attention.

However, Mr. Masters, who was scratching the top of his head again, responded without noticeable enthusiasm, "I'd like to see it some other time; but right now, I'm just too busy."

"I mentioned it," Giraffe went on, "because, if we asked him, Billy might make some such change in a car for Allison, so she could travel with me to Montana."

This did get Mr. Masters's attention, and he began to swing his arms from side to side, the way he often did when he became excited. "When I spoke to Billy about this," Giraffe continued, "he came up with quite a few good ideas. Billy's very creative: he built the Montana railroad—with some help from his friends, of course."

"What did he propose?" Mr. Masters asked, bobbing his head up and down attentively.

"He plans, if you and Allison both agree to the idea of her making this Montana experiment," Giraffe answered, "to create a sort of bathtub on wheels." And he explained to Mr. Masters how Billy might turn a whole railroad car into a shallow pool for Allison and put a fish trough at one end. "I'll be in the very next car," Giraffe assured Mr. Masters, "and I'll be sure she gets her vitamins—that is, of course, if you will be kind enough to supply them to me."

And so it was decided, if Allison should like the idea: Giraffe was insistent on this. "Surely, surely," Mr. Masters agreed, swinging his arms from side to side. "Here, Giraffe," he said grandly, "have a banana." He gestured toward a big stalk, which he always kept hanging up in his office. Giraffe declined, but with great politeness: it was not the right time to offend Mr. Masters the manager.

❄ ❄ ❄

An hour later the foreman of the reptile house introduced Giraffe to Allison. At any rate, he let Giraffe into Allison's home—or what he called her home. Allison, who was too shy to greet her visitor, dug her nose into the mud behind her log.

"Good morning, madam," Giraffe said in a very courtly way to his reluctant hostess: "How are you?" After a pause, when Allison failed to lift her head, he continued: "What a convenient log you have, my dear; you can rest behind it in perfect privacy—even with that big glass window over there."

"Yes," Allison responded with a timid mutter, "I need it."

"I bet my friend, Casper the crocodile, would enjoy such a situation," Giraffe continued. "He has what he describes as a patio for basking beside the pond in Montana where he makes his home. But no cypress log."

Giraffe thought he detected a little response in Allison: she seemed to be waving her tail in a friendly way. But he wasn't sure how to proceed. When he saw it was up to him, however, he bowed his head and said: "I hope you are not offended to be in the company of a great awkward fellow like me." Allison seemed to shake her head, but she didn't look up. "Casper once pointed out," Giraffe continued, "that I am a rather ungainly being, with my long neck and my odd-length legs."

"Is he so critical a person?" Allison asked as she raised up her head a little bit.

"Well," Giraffe responded, "I don't have the sleek, elegant body he has. And look at my hoofs: they're so big and clumsy I can easily get one stuck in a bucket, if I'm not careful; and then, I'm all over spots."

"Does Casper complain about that, too?" Allison murmured, raising her head a little more and looking back toward her visitor. "Crocodiles are so proud."

"There's some sense to what he says," Giraffe replied. "And look at these silly horns on my head. What are they good for?"

"Oh, Giraffe," Allison responded, finally lifting her head clear of the mud, "I don't care what Casper says: you're a beautiful person, so tall and interesting and graceful."

"Graceful?" Giraffe said with a toss of his head. "You should talk to my niece, Eugenia, about being graceful."

"But she's just a child," Allison replied.

"True," Giraffe admitted, "but she's all over spots the same as me: and it won't get any better when she grows up; she'll always have horns, too."

"But that is just the way giraffes are," Allison answered, and she turned around for the first time and examined her visitor closely.

"Casper says the same thing," Giraffe replied, "especially when he sees I'm feeling a little awkward or depressed."

"Casper is right about that," Allison said. "You are a perfect giraffe, and the handsomest one I ever saw."

He was in fact the only giraffe she had ever seen, or so Giraffe suspected. But he went on anyway, taking Allison's compliment as she had meant it: "I've always been satisfied with my looks," he said, "strange as they are. True, I've sometimes envied the lithe, shapely figure you and Casper the crocodile can boast of"—and Giraffe thought he saw a blush start at the tip of Allison's tail and rise all the way up to her muddy snub nose.

But she interrupted him: "Oh, Giraffe, how can you talk so? Look at this nose of mine! I don't know how you might feel about it, I mean, after I've cleaned the mud off it, of course;" and she gave Giraffe a little smile. "But what about your friend, Casper the crocodile? What would he say?"

"If you should find yourself beside Casper's pond in Montana someday," Giraffe answered, "the first thing he'd do is invite you to join him for a picnic; and I hope you would accept. The next thing he'd do, after you and he had shared the fresh trout, bass, and pike his pond provides, is to tell you how lonely he is—or, rather, how lonely he was until your visit. Then he'd show you his patio and invite you to climb up and bask."

"I doubt that, Giraffe," Allison responded, although, as Giraffe noticed, she was breathing almost too hard to speak. "He would start by noticing my nose, just like those crocodiles in the next room: look at them yawn."

"Maybe," Giraffe acknowledged: "Casper is proud of what he himself calls his 'elegant nose.' But maybe not. For one thing: his best friend is Hal the hippo whose nose—of which he's rather vain, by the way—is as snubbed as yours. For another: Casper is a gracious person, and a very lonely one. He's actually invited Hal to climb up and bask beside him." Then Giraffe told Allison about the conversation at the pond.

"You know, Allison, my dear, we all have the kinds of bodies we have: I have my horns and my spots and my big feet; you have your snub nose and your beautiful white scales."

"But do you think Casper would really like me, Giraffe?"

"I can't be sure," Giraffe answered. "I myself admire you; and, as you may have noticed, I have a nose that is almost as long and altogether as distinguished as Casper's;" and he cocked his head so Allison could get the full effect of his fine profile. "Why not join me on the Montana train and pay Casper a little visit? Then we'll see."

"A little visit?" Allison said. "You must know, Giraffe, once I leave my house here at the zoo, I can never return. Mr. Masters the manager will install some more accommodating alligators to replace me; he has as good as told me so. And I can't really blame him," Allison went on: "I've been a real failure here at the zoo."

"That may be true," Giraffe replied, "but things are different in Montana."

"Yes, I can imagine," Allison responded. "But what if I don't fit in? What if I'm just as much of a failure there—and just as unhappy?"

"You could hardly be worse off than you are here in the zoo," Giraffe suggested.

"I could be colder," Allison said with a little shudder.

Then Giraffe told her about the improvements Casper had made in his winter quarters; he told her how Casper stiffened up comfortably in the Montana winter; and how he thawed in the spring sunshine. He didn't mention how Casper yawned so broadly when he first awoke that, as Hal the hippo once observed, you could count every one of his teeth; but he did tell Allison how Casper came out of the pond after his first fishing expedition each spring and complained there were too many fish for any one person to eat.

"But what if Casper doesn't like me, Giraffe? What if he just doesn't want to share the pond with me? What if he would be embarrassed to bask in my company?"

"Then, my dear, you and I will get on the Montana train and come straight back to sunny Florida. There are plenty of spots here—cypress swamps and fishy marshes and warm pools—where a fine alligator like you could be perfectly comfortable. And I promise to help you discover one, if you find Montana doesn't suit you."

That settled the matter. It was not so much Giraffe's guarantee, however, as his friendship that made Allison take a chance on Montana. Because of his amiable, sympathetic manners—and not really because of her confidence in the life she would lead in such a cold, mountainous state—Allison decided to give Montana a chance, fearful as she was about being scorned by his elegant friend.

The trip back to Montana was both uneventful and comfortable. Billy the beaver made Allison the bathtub car Giraffe had described to Mr. Masters the manager, and he filled the trough with the kind of fish he knew she was used to. He cut a window between her car and Giraffe's so they could visit and so Giraffe could dispense the vitamins Mr. Masters had furnished for the trip. The foreman of the reptile house failed to show up to see Allison off; and even her personal attendant stayed away; but Mr. Masters, despite his busy schedule, did come down to the station. He bade her and Giraffe an elaborate farewell, raising his hand first to scratch his head and then to wave at the departing travelers. He had had a whole stalk of bananas placed in Giraffe's car in case Giraffe should become hungry for a banana along the way. The last Giraffe saw of Mr. Masters the manager as the train rolled away, he was bobbing his head up and down and swinging his arms from side to side.

During a brief pause in Lexington so Billy the beaver could take on more coal and water, Giraffe was able to buy a picture of Henry Clay's home. And as they crossed "the father of waters," while Allison was sleeping, he had a chance to look for a spot he might bring her to if things didn't work out in Montana. Giraffe was more worried about this than he had admitted to either Allison or Mr. Masters. He had sent an e-mail message to Princess Isabel before leaving Florida: "I will arrive on Wednesday—with a visitor, a guest for Casper the crocodile. Ask him to prepare a picnic lunch and, if he feels up to it, to scramble over to the station to greet us. Love, Giraffe." He was sure the princess would fulfill his request, and he expected Casper to be at the station to welcome Allison although it meant a big effort—maybe two big efforts—for his friend.

As large a delegation was on hand to greet the travelers as Giraffe had hoped for. Casper was a very hospitable crocodile, and with a big audience observing him, or so Giraffe believed, he would feel obliged to play the gracious host. News of Giraffe's return had spread all over Montana: it was not everyday anybody there received e-mail. Everyone anticipated the arrival of the "visitor," and almost everyone asked Princess Isabel who it might be. Princess Isabel would have been happy to tell—if only she had known. Giraffe was a clever one. As it was, the assembled citizens of Montana simply had to wait. The most anxious of them all was Casper, who was sporting a beautiful white sash for the occasion. He had reached the station almost an hour before the train was due. And since it was—like all trains—an hour late, Casper had had a chance to become very nervous. Before leaving the pond, he had brushed his teeth with special care and even flossed them with catfish whiskers; he had asked Hal the hippo to inspect him—twice; and he had laid out an elegant lunch with an eel he had just caught coiled at the center of his appetizing display. But still he felt nervous.

"Be calm, like me, old friend," Ella the elephant

counseled, as she ambled up to him; but you can imagine how much that helped.

She arrived carrying Rudolph the raccoon, who was waving a banner, "Welcome home, Giraffe." She was holding a flag in her trunk, which said the same thing; and she had tied a big red balloon to her tail. Both Leo and Lucy the lions strolled over, looking very majestic. Kanga, who had left Roo playing with the little possums, brought another jar of honey. And although it was too close to Christmas for Rudolf the red-nosed reindeer to attend, Zane and Zack the zebras trotted up wearing their imitation antlers.

Gloria the gorilla, who dropped off a cask of her famous banana punch at the pond on her way to the station—"in case the travelers should need a little pick-me-up"—had encountered Dr. Oscar the orangutan along the path; and the two of them arrived together. Dr. Oscar was carrying his medical bag, of course, just in case. Hal the hippo stayed back at the pond making sure everything was perfect for the picnic; and Princess Isabel and Isabel remained at the palace, despite a strong curiosity to see Casper's guest. They planned to pay a visit to the pond in a day or two when she—somehow they'd found this out—had had a chance to catch her breath: this was Isabel's idea. Even so there was quite a crowd assembled to welcome Giraffe and Allison.

Giraffe was the first one off the train after Billy the beaver finally brought it to a stop: he had planned this with Allison, who was shy about meeting so many new faces—even if they were, as Giraffe had explained to her, all friendly ones. He trotted down the gangplank to great acclaim.

The gibbering and hooting and growling and grunt-ing and whinnying that greeted Giraffe would have startled a more confident person than Allison. But after Giraffe had greeted his friends and absorbed their vociferous excitement, a hush fell over them all, like the hush in a theater when the curtain is about to go up. This did not altogether reassure Allison, who had been quaking in a far corner of her car while Giraffe was being welcomed home. And when Billy the beaver lowered the gangplank, there was no one there—or so it seemed. Giraffe, who understood what Allison was feeling, went up to the door of her car, taking Kanga, a sympathetic person, along with him. They both assured Allison she was among folks every one of whom wanted to be her friend, and she had nothing to fear.

But she was afraid, all the same, very afraid. And all the inhabitants of Montana saw for several seconds was a few feet of her glistening white tail—the same sight she had pre-sented to the kids at the Florida Zoo. It was enough to make Casper's heart beat a little quicker, but Ella and Rudolph and Gloria and all the other folks who had come to the station to welcome the visitor were still in a state of suspense. Luckily the train lurched, the way trains do sometimes, and Allison found herself suddenly deposited in Montana.

When she realized where she was and felt all the curious eyes gazing at her, Allison blushed a bright glowing pink from the tapered tip of her tail to the end of her nose: she was a beautiful sight.

Everybody gasped; but Casper, although he was more affected than anyone else, immediately seized his responsibility as the host and, scrambling forward as fast as his claws would carry him, said in an extremely gallant manner: "Greetings, madam. My friends and I have come to the station especially to welcome you to Montana."

Allison felt herself blushing even more, but not entirely, as she herself began to recognize, from fear and embarrassment.

"I have prepared a little repast for you, with the help of my friends," Casper continued, "and if you will allow me the pleasure, I will accompany you to my humble abode down at the pond where, if you will be so kind, we may feast and relax." Allison had never been addressed with such elegance before, not even by Giraffe, and she found that she liked it. Giraffe, who had listened to Casper with great but diminishing anxiety, was very proud of his friend—and very relieved.

Allison and Casper scrambled together toward the pond, with Giraffe, who had waited back to visit a little bit with his old friends, trailing comfortably along behind. The folks of Montana were all sensitive to the feelings of other people—except for Rudolph the raccoon, whose enthusiasm sometimes got the better of him; they realized at once that Allison was shy, although the reason for it escaped them. And so they left the station with a minimum of whinnying, growling, jibbering, snorting, and cheeping and allowed Allison and Casper, the guest of honor and her escort, to depart quietly without facing the many questions about Giraffe's trip and his lovely companion that were in fact troubling them mightily.

The first thing Giraffe heard when he caught up to Casper and Allison was her description of Mr. Masters: "When he's pleased with anything," she was explaining to her companion, "he swings his arms from side to side, like this;" and she gave a better impression of this mannerism than you might have expected. "When he's satisfied with anybody," she continued, "he offers a banana. He gave one to Giraffe's niece, Eugenia, because she was such a good sport about getting her foot caught in a bucket. And he presented Giraffe a whole stalk for bringing me out of Florida.

"Oh, Giraffe," she said, when she realized he had overtaken them, "I've held us all up by talking so much. But we don't move very fast at the best, do we, Casper?"

"You should ask Casper about his victory last year in the great Olympic race over at the palace grounds, shouldn't she, Casper? He moved fast that day."

"Oh, Casper," Allison said, "please tell me all about it."

"I'll be happy to and, if you like, to show you my medal," Casper replied. "But here we are at the pond—I hope you like it—and here is the lunch Hal the hippo has been preparing for us, and here is Hal." Indeed, Hal had just emerged from the bottom of the pond and come into view beside the picnic spot. "Hal, my dear friend," Casper said, "may I introduce you to my guest, Allison the alligator?"

The picnic, which Casper and Hal had situated right beside their pond, was very cheery. Allison and her eager host feasted on a variety of fresh fish. Allison, who had never eaten eel before, was shy about it at first, but, with a little encouragement from Casper, she tried a bit of the tail and was soon sharing the whole succulent length of it with great relish. Hal wallowed in the pond right beside his three companions, ducking down to scrape up some green slime for himself and then bobbing up again. Giraffe found a pile of delectable leaves gathered—by magic?—and skillfully arranged at his place; and he fed heartily. The trip, during which he made do on quite dry and withered fare, had given him an excellent appetite.

Hal's bobbing up and down reminded Allison of Mr. Masters the manager's way of bobbing his head up and down to emphasize a point, and she gave an amusing account of that: "Haven't I got it about right, Giraffe?" she asked, after attempting an impression.

"Yes, you're pretty close," Giraffe agreed. "It especially reminds me of the time he explained to me you would be too slow to thrive in Montana. He thinks our state is nothing but woods and mountains and empty space."

"Let me tell you," Hal exclaimed with a snort, "he didn't know Allison would find a speedy Olympian up here who would help her adjust."

"Oh, Casper," Allison exclaimed, as she swallowed her last bite of eel, "please tell me how you won the Montana Olympics: you promised you would." And, after a little encouragement, Casper did, describing the event and his

39

success with what Giraffe approved as becoming candor.

There was a pause when he had finished and, with the assistance of Giraffe, demonstrated his medal. After admiring it, Allison sighed and said she needed a dip to soak the soot from the train out of her scales. "Afterwards," she said, "I wonder if there is a beach someplace where I might bask for a while."

"Of course," Casper responded. "My patio is over there"—pointing a little way up the bank of the pond with his nose: "There's plenty of basking room for two, that is, for the two of us, if you would do me the honor of your company."

"Gladly," Allison replied, and then, after thanking Hal for the picnic and giving Giraffe a lovely smile, she slid gracefully into the pond.

As Giraffe turned to go to his cave, Hal nodded at him, and the two friends exchanged a congratulatory glance.

Casper accompanied Giraffe down the path to have a chat with him. "Thank you, my dear friend," he began, "for introducing me to this lovely alligator."

"She is sweet, isn't she?" Giraffe said.

"And such a witty, amusing talker," Casper added.

"Yes," Giraffe agreed, "although that is a side of her I'd never seen before today at the picnic. But tell me," he went on before Casper could respond, "how did Hal gather the pile of leaves he served me?" It was something he had wondered about all the time he was eating.

"I can't imagine," Casper replied. And the two of them had a good laugh at the idea of Hal the hippo scrambling up the trunk of an elm or an oak to fetch his friend a lunch of nice tender leaves. But Casper couldn't think for long of anyone but Allison. "She's so gracious a person," he exclaimed. "She was uneasy about my eel at first, could you tell? But once she tried it, she ate almost as much as I did. And such beautiful teeth! Did you notice, Giraffe?"

"Yes," Giraffe replied, canceling his anxiety about Allison's snub nose once for all: "She should be an excellent addition to our society here in Montana. I hope she decides to stay."

"Me, too," said Casper.

That night, as Giraffe lay down to sleep, he remembered the beavers, who had covered the main room of his cave with wall to wall moss. He inhaled the cedar from the fire Rudolph the raccoon, an expert on fires and fireplaces, had laid and lighted at his cave's mouth especially to welcome him home. He gazed around with satisfaction at the walls of his room: it was good to be back. There seemed to be the faint scent of banana in the air, and as Giraffe wondered sleepily about it, he detected the hint of snow he knew he'd find outside his front door in the morning—and for many mornings afterwards. This brought the problem of the Christmas tree to mind. "But," he murmured with a yawn, "I'll think about that tomorrow." Instead, he thought about Allison the alligator. Giraffe felt sure, as he considered everything that had happened in the past few weeks, Casper would make her comfortable in what he hoped would be her new home. Then Giraffe thought drowsily about the Christmas present for Princess Isabel, a pair of plaid gloves which Rudolf the red-nosed reindeer had brought him from the North Pole, and the Christmas present he himself had brought back from Florida for Isabel, a green t-shirt with a picture of Mr. Masters the manager on the front.

Such good friends. As he fell asleep, he whispered to himself, "I'm the luckiest giraffe in Montana."

Olympics

❄ ❄ ❄

Allison the alligator had just finished the last bite of the eel, which Casper the crocodile provided for the picnic that introduced her to Montana; and, before Giraffe or Hal the hippo, the other guests, could say goodbye, she turned to Casper and asked him to tell her about the Montana Olympics: "You promised, Casper," she reminded him, "and

I am very eager to hear about your victory."

"Yes," said Giraffe, "I heard you give Allison such a promise. And so did Hal, didn't you, Hal?"

"Yes, I believe so," Hal replied, "and it seems to me, let me tell you, this is the perfect time to make good on it. What do you say, Casper?"

"I will be happy to," Casper responded, "if you fellows will stick around and make sure I don't leave out anything. Actually, Giraffe, you organized the event: maybe you should describe it."

"No, no, Casper," cried Allison, "you promised: Giraffe will listen and make sure you get it right, won't you, Giraffe?"

"It's Casper's victory," Hal put in, "he should describe it. Besides, I'm sure Allison would prefer to hear about it from his own lips, don't you agree, Giraffe?"

"Yes," said Giraffe, "it's your story, Casper—and your promise."

"Very well," replied the courtly crocodile, "I will give the best account I can."

❄ ❄ ❄

"That spring everybody in Montana became excited about the international Olympics scheduled to be held in Billings, and somebody had the bright idea"—

"It was Rudolph the raccoon, in fact," murmured Giraffe.

"That Rudolph," said Hal.

"Okay, then, Rudolph the raccoon had the bright idea we should hold our own Olympics, a Montana Olympics, isn't that right, Giraffe? Everybody approved the idea, including King Cole; and almost everybody had a suggestion about the competition.

"Billy the beaver advocated a tree-felling contest, naturally, and Kanga urged the long jump. The other beavers and the raccoons suggested fishing until they remembered me. Rudolf the red-nosed reindeer, partly because he was busy at the North Pole, did not request a race up in the air; but Marvin the mole did try to get some support for a race down under the ground. 'It's not fair,' he complained, 'to make me compete where I can't see.'

"Balleau the bear wanted a wrestling match, an idea that appealed to Fergus the footman's son—he wrestled for Harvard, you know. And Dr. Oscar the orangutan requested a race through the trees. 'Why not a bandaging contest, doctor?' Rudolph the raccoon asked him during one of our arguments."

"That Rudolph!" said Hal.

"What kind of competition did you vote for, Hal," asked Allison, "log-rolling?" Everybody laughed, and then Casper went on.

"For some days it seemed we would never be able to agree, but finally Giraffe, Princess Isabel and the king, our Olympic Committee, met and decided. The princess had hoped to establish synchronized swimming, a terrible idea; but luckily for us all, her sister was afraid of the water, and the princess couldn't find anyone to team up with. 'I wish the otters had immigrated,' she once said to you, Giraffe, didn't she?"

"Yes," Giraffe replied, "but, since no otters were available, she came to agree with the king and me on a cross-country race."

"She actually approached me about teaming up with her. The princess in synchronized swimming with a crocodile: wouldn't we have been a sight?

"But the Olympic Committee decided on a race and chose a course which seemed to you three to give everybody a chance—everybody but me, at any rate."

"Everybody but Marvin, you mean, Casper," Giraffe said defensively: "There was a good stretch of water."

"A stretch of water? The creek running through the palace grounds! When I first heard about it, I twitched from the tip of my nose to the tip of my tail!"

"It was enough to discourage Leo the lion," Giraffe explained, "not to speak of Marvin the mole."

"And even Kanga complained a little, let me tell you," added Hal.

"The course the Committee chose for us, at any rate, originated in the woods at the south side of the palace grounds; it struck straight through the palace meadow for a few hundred yards, then went down a steep bank to The Great Missouri Creek—The Great Missouri Creek, what a laugh!—across the creek, maybe a fifty-yard swim; up the long slope at the other side; and then another hundred yards of meadow through the palace gate."

"That bank," Giraffe explained, "really tested Zane, the faster of the zebras, and completely discouraged Ella the elephant."

"It totally ruined my chances of competing," said Hal with a sigh.

"Oh, Hal," Allison asked, "what happened?"

"I was practicing my descent down the bank, which was just as much a problem for me, let me tell you," Hal explained, "as it was for Zane. My friend, Rudolph the raccoon, our expert on that section of the course, was coaching me. You may sniff, Casper, with your long nose, but at least he was encouraging me."

"He was encouraging you, all right. I had just reached the bank after a good stiff scramble through the meadow, and I could see Rudolph talking away at you."

"He was trying to help," Hal insisted.

"Oh yes, to help you tumble down the bank."

"I asked him to advise me: sliding down was so easy for him. I am fairly graceful on level ground, much nimbler, in fact, than you might expect, Allison, but the bank worried me; and Rudolph thought he could help."

"He helped you all right, as I observed while I was catching my breath: he helped you almost break your neck."

"Actually," Giraffe interrupted, "Rudolph became very frightened, Casper, when Hal lost his balance and went down. I could hear him crying out from where I was standing on the other side of the creek, 'Watch that rock, Hal, watch that rock!' And when you fell, Hal, he rushed down so fast he almost fell on top of you. 'Hal,' he cried, 'are you okay?' And while I was carrying Dr. Oscar the orangutan over the creek to attend you, as both of you surely remember, Rudolph was saying loud enough even for me to hear, as I splashed through the water, 'I shouldn't have let him try the bank; I should have stopped him.'

"Do you remember, Casper, how frightened he was for his friend?"

"Yes, I do, Giraffe. It was pitiful the way he kept asking Dr. Oscar, 'Is Hal going to be all right, doctor,' as he rubbed his eyes with his tail: 'will he be all right?'"

"I saw him, too," Giraffe said, "and it's the only time I ever saw Rudolph do such a thing. But it did look like Hal had hurt himself pretty badly."

"How badly did you hurt yourself, Hal?" asked Allison.

"Oh," Hal replied, "it looked worse than it was."

"The sight of our hippo tumbling down the rocky bank," Giraffe insisted, "really scared all of us, didn't it, Casper?"

"Yes, I must admit, it scared me."

"Hal landed with a thump," Giraffe said as if he was hearing it again: "It seemed to shake the ground all the way over on my side of the creek."

"I wasn't hurt very badly," Hal said, "except for my pride."

"Your ankle was so sprained," Giraffe contradicted him, "Dr. Oscar officially scratched you from the race. And everybody was upset."

"Very true, Giraffe," agreed Casper. "I myself saw Ella, who had been standing with me at the bank's edge when you fell, Hal, swing her trunk from side to side for two or three minutes and then, with a snort, turn back to the meadow."

"And that swim," Giraffe continued, "it frightened Leo, the king of beasts, so much that his wife, Lucy, finally had to represent him and all the lions."

"It would have frightened Gloria, too, as you are about to remind me," Casper said, "if there hadn't been a grove of alders at the creek, the branches of which allowed her—and Peter o'Possum, if he wanted to—to swing across."

"We tried to choose a course, Allison," Giraffe insisted, "which would give every participant in the race a decent chance. The creek was wider than Casper remembers, and it flowed pretty fast."

"Just ask Giraffe this, Allison: did Rudolph snicker when I said I planned to enter the race? Did Bo Bo and Lucy mock what they called my 'easy running gait' when we were all working out in the meadow together the week before the race? Didn't Kanga—even Kanga—have a little laughing fit when she and Peter considered my chances of winning?"

"But you entered, anyway," said Hal, "and I really admired your spunk; I did, Allison, let me tell you, I admired Casper's spunk."

"It was Giraffe who made me enter, wasn't it, Giraffe? 'Winning isn't important, Casper,' you said, 'competing is what matters.'"

"I did say that—to you, Casper, and to all the people

in Montana. I only wish I could have competed."

"You might have won, too, Giraffe," said Hal, "with those long graceful legs of yours. I watched you exercise during the early days before the king appointed you President of the Olympics and commanded you to give up the race, and I thought you might take it. Once you got going during the try-outs, you galloped right by Bo Bo and Lucy and even Zane."

"No, Hal," Giraffe replied, "I would have floundered in the creek just like Zane did. But it was fun to anticipate the competition and to practice over the course, wasn't it, Casper?"

"Yes, although I knew I didn't have a chance, I scrambled across the meadow with pleasure, and it was great fun for me sliding down the bank into the creek—but not for Zane. Poor Zane, he never quite fell down like Hal, but he was always awkward and insecure scooting down on that striped butt of his. Of course, Peter and Rudolph, both of whom are pretty fast runners, slid down it almost as easily as I did; and they were good swimmers, too—"

"But not as strong as you, Casper," murmured Giraffe.

"I thought the race would be settled between the two of them," Casper said.

"So did Rudolph," said Hal. "You remember, Giraffe, he started booking bets on the race—"

"That Rudolph," muttered Giraffe.

"—and listed himself as the favorite: at two-to-one."

"Yes," Casper said, "and ask Hal, Allison, at what odds Rudolph listed me, just ask him."

"Well, Hal," Allison asked, "what were the odds on Casper?"

"Five-hundred-to-one," Hal replied, "but it was just a joke because nobody bet on Casper."

"I would have," said Allison, "if I had been here."

"No, you wouldn't have," Giraffe responded, "because King Cole forbade any betting on the race. It would have been contrary to the Olympic spirit."

"Yes, yes, Giraffe," Casper agreed, "it wasn't winning but competing that mattered, right?"

"That's right, Casper, and you had already won a victory just by competing."

"You were so heroic, Casper," exclaimed Allison. "I would never have been brave enough even to try."

"Well, I thought the reptiles should at least be represented, although I knew I couldn't win one of the medals."

"Medals." Allison asked, "what medals?"

"The king had three medals struck in Missoula, a gold for the winner of the race, a silver for second, and a bronze for third. They were designed by a professor of sculpture at the university, an old classmate of his. On the front of each one was an image of Montana with a sun shining behind it; and on the back was a bust of the king with the motto, *Splendide Rex*, underneath."

"Oh," Allison exclaimed, "I wish I could see one of those."

"You will," Giraffe assured her with a smile: "You will."

❄ ❄ ❄

"The preliminaries in the weeks leading up to the competition were very exciting, weren't they, Giraffe?"

"Yes, Casper, those were some of the most wonderful weeks I've ever known."

"We competitors," Casper went on, "would assemble informally in the palace meadow every day to strengthen ourselves and to practice what was for each of us the hardest part of the course. Poor Zane had to work at sliding down the bank—with Zack's coaching."

"Actually, Allison," Giraffe interrupted, "Zane was very brave."

"True, Giraffe, true," Casper agreed, "it was a hazard for him. I remember Zack shouting up at him as he started to scoot, 'Keep your hooves down, Zane, or you'll lose your balance. Hooves down! Hooves down!' as poor Zane tipped sideways and slid down to the bottom of the bank. 'Hooves down!' became kind of a joke after a while. When Gloria was losing her grip on an alder branch up above the creek one morning, Rudolph, who was cavorting in the water below, cried out, 'Hooves down, Gloria, hooves down!' and everybody—except Dr. Oscar the orangutan, who was coaching her—laughed out loud. He just threw his arms up in the air and bellowed, 'You'll never win the race, Gloria, if you don't always hold on with your trailing hand while you swing ahead.' 'Well, doctor,' Gloria grunted to herself as she crawled out of the creek, 'maybe you should represent the apes.'

"But he couldn't, of course, because he had to be on call in case of injuries. And there were injuries, too, although nothing really serious except for Hal's. Gloria drank too much banana punch one morning—'Building up my courage for the alders,' she explained—and developed a case of indigestion; Balleau suffered more than once from heat exhaustion; Kanga got some mud in her pouch; and I scratched my nose climbing up the slope on the far side of the creek."

"Actually," Hal interrupted him, "you bumped it on a big rock; and it really swelled up, Allison, let me tell you."

"I admit, whatever you or Giraffe may tell us, Hal, that it became a little swollen, but only for a few days," Casper said, "and, look, Allison, it didn't leave any scar at all. It was nothing to the scrapes and bruises poor Zane had to endure, sliding down to the creek.

"Lucy and Kanga spent most of their time helping one another to practice crossing. Kanga took two or three big hops every time as she approached the bank and then launched herself out over the water, but she always flopped with a great splash. 'Hooves down, hooves down,' muttered Rudolph as he paddled around observing her. 'You'd do better,' Lucy roared at Kanga from the bank above, 'if you wouldn't insist on carrying Roo.' 'Roo and I go together, always, don't we, Roo?' Kanga sputtered as she struggled to get her footing. 'But he's gotten too big to be carried around,' Lucy growled, 'especially in a race. Roo's almost too big to be a cowboy, isn't he, Peter?' Lucy asked the possum, who always watched Kanga's aquatic exercise. 'Can't you talk some sense into her?' 'Roo helps me keep my balance, don't you, Roo?' Kanga insisted. 'I would be glad to nurse Roo for you,' Peter suggested, 'if I wasn't entered in the race myself.'

'But you are, dear sir, and besides, Roo and I really belong together, don't we, Roo?' and that settled it.

"Lucy's problems crossing the creek were different from Kanga's. From infancy she had been told lions hate water, and she had never thought to question it, so she entered the creek at first very timidly, one paw at a time. 'Go on, go on,' the ever-present Rudolph encouraged her, 'it's not so bad—if you keep your hooves down. Here, watch me.' And he plunged in, splashing about until he soaked both Kanga and Lucy. 'Rudolph, Rudolph,' the two ladies cried out, 'you stop that!'

"The funny thing was though, unlike Kanga, who always hated getting wet, Lucy really liked the water. After a few days she leaped into the creek without pausing and, although she never became a really good swimmer, she paddled around very happily. This disgusted Leo, who lounged well up the slope on the palace side of the creek, watching with Larry and Lola: 'Your mother has a little tiger blood in her veins,' he would tell them, 'just as I have always suspected.' It affected Rudolph the raccoon, who was still planning to book bets on the race, quite differently: he lowered Lucy's odds from thirty-to-one to thirteen-to-two. She was, of course, a very good runner, although not as fast as Zane."

"Rudolph was planning," Giraffe said, interrupting the train of Casper's narrative, "to erect a gambling booth between the Olympic stands and the palace—"

"That Rudolph," muttered Hal.

"—and he had trained Ruth the raccoon, his loving

wife, in all the fine points of book-making. The king and the Olympic Committee quashed those plans."

"Rudolph also lowered my odds," Casper said, "when he saw how seriously I was training for the running leg of the race. Balleau the bear and I worked out together nearly every day. Balleau was a lot faster than me—at least when we started out: he would lumber off and leave me in the dust. But he was in such bad shape he became quite exhausted before he got to the creek; and, scrambling along, using my tail to extend my back legs—as I learned to do— I would pass him by every time. Once, after watching me pass Balleau and get ready to shinny down the bank, Rudolph sidled up to me and murmured, so no one else could hear, he was lowering the odds on me way down to one-hundred-to-one—quite a compliment!"

"Poor Balleau," said Giraffe, "the weight he worked off every morning he put back on every night. He never could control his appetite; besides, I don't believe he took the Olympics as seriously as the rest of you."

"All of us were serious," Casper said. "When Gloria wasn't practicing swinging through the branches of the alders along the creek, she raced around the meadow, training with Lucy and Kanga—and Roo. After a while, although she tried to model her running style on Lucy, she hopped along a lot like Kanga—pretty funny. But all three of them trained hard to strengthen themselves for the race. Of course Zane could gallop past and around any of us—even Lucy. But he had such trouble with the bank of The Great Missouri Creek that his victory was never assured. Rudolph listed him, in fact, at eight-to-one—higher odds than he listed on Lucy once she learned to swim.

"Rudolph had gotten it into his head, however, the race was between himself and Peter o'Possum; and they were shifty performers, both of them. They scurried around the meadow tirelessly, outrunning everybody but Zane. And the bank, with which he never learned to cope, poor Zane, was no problem for either of them. But the slope on the other side of the creek, which was very muddy and slippery, gave most of us participants, including Peter, a lot of trouble. Poor Zane could hardly get his hooves under him, and even Lucy sometimes slipped: I remember her sliding all the way down one time and going right into the water, and that was before she learned to swim. It was pitiful to watch Kanga—and Roo—try to hop up the slope. But Rudolph scampered up it with no trouble at all: his claws fixed firmly in the muddy going. Bo Bo was pretty sure-footed, too. The beavers had chosen him over Billy, whose fat tail made him run with a waddle, although, as it turned out, Bo Bo was not, even with his scrawny tail, much faster than Billy. I had no trouble with the slope either; but, of course, I crept up it a lot slower than Rudolph did. It seemed like two-to-one was a fair estimate of his chances.

"But there was one problem for Rudolph—and for most of the participants in the race: the strong current of The Great Missouri Creek. He and Peter and Bo Bo, who could have used more fat in his tail when he was in the water, were all swept downstream while they swam, especially when they practiced swimming after a rain."

"True," Giraffe interrupted with satisfaction, "you see, Allison, the course proved to be fairer even under normal conditions than Casper wants to admit."

"But under normal conditions, Rudolph was forced only a few yards downstream, not far enough to make much difference, isn't that right, Giraffe? And there didn't seem to be any chance I could overtake even Peter or Bo Bo."

❄ ❄ ❄

"The day of the race dawned sunny and bright," Casper continued. "There were thick clouds on the western horizon, and Dr. Neil Frank promised a heavy rain by evening, but the day, after a spell of wet weather, looked almost perfect.

"The king had erected two stands between his palace and the great front gate, which was going to serve as the finish line for the race: one for himself and for the other Olympic officials, the other, at the top of which was a platform with three levels, for the presentation of the Olympic medals. The royal stand he ordered to be painted purple, the presentation stand, gold."

"A little excessive, I thought," Giraffe muttered.

"Two flags flew above the royal stand: the Montana flag, which is forty shades of green; and the Olympic flag with its interconnected circles. The presentation stand was decorated with cascades of colorful streamers. Nearer The Great Missouri Creek, the king had ordered the beavers, under the direction of Oscar the footman, to erect a fine, large viewing stand to accommodate the citizens of Montana.

"All around these three stands were booths for sweets and drinks and sandwiches—but not for betting. In one booth, Marian the maid, who had powdered her pretty nose for the occasion, was serving honey; in another, Patsy o'Possum was serving mead; and in a third, young raccoons and possums were offering fried fish on the queen's own bread. A catering company had put up a large tent behind the stand for the spectators and was dispensing cotton candy, sasparilla, sherbet, chocolate ants, and pine gum—all at the king's expense. There were also rides scattered here and there: a carousel, a dodgem track, and, for the daring, a shaky ferris wheel. And games: a ducking tank—operated mostly by Billy and the beavers; an apple tub—operated by Ella, who was determined to help; a chance to pin a tail on the dragon; and another, to pin a tail on the king of Idaho. At the great front gate the three fiddlers King Cole had called up from Tennessee just for the Olympics were playing 'The Forest Walks of Montana,' 'Montana, Here I Come,' 'My Old Montana Home,' 'Montana, My Montana,' and other appropriate music.

"The crowd, which had gathered from all over the state, was very festive. In addition to the locals, there were goats and sheep from the mountains, armadillos and porcupines from the south, wolverines and sloths from the deep woods, and, from the eastern end of the state, a couple of King Arthur's knights in full armor. If the stands had not been so big and so well-built—fashioned from seasoned lumber and fastened with twine—they could not have supported this throng—especially during the excitement of the race.

"When race time came, all us participants stood in a line on the other side of the creek at the top of the bank while Giraffe, speaking through a megaphone, introduced each one individually:

> '*Zane the zebra*, representing all the hooved and all the striped inhabitants of Africa and Asia;
>
> '*Balleau the bear*, representing the bears of all colors and sizes around the globe, including pandas;
>
> '*Gloria the gorilla*, representing the gibbons, chimpanzees, orangutans and all great apes;
>
> '*Kanga and Roo*, representing England and Australia;
>
> '*Lucy the lion*, representing all the cats of the world, and chiefly the female cats;
>
> '*Peter o'Possum*, representing the marsupials of North and South America;
>
> '*Casper the Crocodile*, representing all walking reptiles, living and extinct;
>
> '*Rudolph the raccoon*, representing all nocturnal creatures, except bats;
>
> '*Bo Bo the beaver*, representing the organic builders of the world.'

"The introduction of each person was greeted with applause: when Lucy's name was announced little Larry the lion got so excited he almost fell out of the stands—to his father's great embarrassment. After Giraffe had made all the introductions, the fiddlers performed 'Hail to the Victors,' a tune they had learned while studying music at the University of Michigan. And everybody cheered.

"We participants recognized King Cole, the Olympic Committee, and the Montana Public, bowing toward each in turn (if you can imagine me bowing); then we turned back into the meadow toward the forest, where Isabel waited with a great gong to start the race; and, while the fiddlers continued to play, we began to loosen up for the challenge to come. The crowd marveled at Zane's smooth gallop and at Lucy's leaping stride as they swept across the meadow; they wondered at Gloria's hobble-de-hop; and they couldn't help laughing as they watched me scrambling and pumping along behind everyone else on my way to the start."

"That wasn't very nice," Allison complained.

"No," Casper said. "And I felt it, too, but you can't really blame them: I did seem badly overmatched; even Balleau lumbered right away from me, at least for a few big steps.

"Isabel, whom the king had chosen to start the race, took her place at the starting line in the woods. Oscar the footman, whom the king had appointed the steward of the first long leg of the race, climbed the little platform that had been built so he could survey all the meadow. The king had invited Rudolf the red-nosed reindeer to survey the run across the meadow from the air, but Rudolf was regrettably unable to attend. Fergus the footman's son launched his motorboat—less to provide surveillance than to prepare for emergencies—and a good thing, too, as it turned out. Princess Isabel stationed herself at the great front gate since her task was to judge the finish. King Cole surveyed the whole course as the master of the competition, and President Giraffe stood beside him for consultation in case any problems should arise.

"A few drops of rain began to fall as we approached Isabel with her gong at the starting line, and the clouds, which had been moving west along The Great Missouri Creek all day, grew very dark above us. But we were all too excited about the race and too concerned, each of us individually, about his own strategy, to pay much attention to the weather. I remember I was especially thinking about using my tail to propel me across the meadow. But Kanga, who disliked water in any form, warned her passenger, 'Keep down in my pouch, Roo, or you'll get wet.' That made us all laugh: we figured Roo was going to get wet all right, one way or another. 'I wonder,' Zane whinnied to himself, 'if this rain will make it any easier for me to get down the bank.' 'Not easy enough,' muttered Rudolph, who was happy to see conditions which seemed to suit him perfectly.

"It was beginning to rain very hard by the time we all got in line; and, just as Isabel struck her gong to start the race, there was a tremendous flash of lightning, a clap of thunder, and suddenly a great curtain of rain came sweeping across the meadow. It didn't much matter that the rain completely hid the creek, the grandstand and the palace: we all knew the way. But it did affect the way we ran.

"Zane had trouble with the downpour and the slippery going, but he led the way to the creek all the same. Balleau also lumbered off in good style until his coat became soaked. Then he gave a great heave of his chest and stopped dead in his tracks so, although I had been trailing everybody, I passed him by much sooner than I had expected. The slippery going, of course, made me feel right at home. The smaller creatures scrambled along almost as well as if the ground were dry; and Rudolph, who reveled in the deepening mud, kept closer to Zane than he ever had in the weeks of training.

"Lucy had little trouble leaping along, but Kanga hopped very timidly and tried, until the whole meadow became a quagmire, to dodge the puddles. Gloria bounced along beside her. The rain was falling so thick and hard Oscar the footman couldn't have seen a foul if there had been one. And Rudolf the red-nosed reindeer, even if he could have kept aloft, would have been as blind as Marvin the mole. The audience in the grandstand, who must have heard the starting gong sound just before the lightning struck, couldn't see anything either, could you, Giraffe?"

"No," Giraffe admitted, "we just waited as the rain poured down, unable to see beyond the bank on the other side of the creek. Before long, in fact, there wasn't any bank: the creek had become a raging torrent, swollen right to the edge of the bank on the far side and almost to the palace gate on ours: it was completely filled by the rushing water that had been falling and draining into it upstream for the whole day. And the meadow beyond was totally invisible."

"The first runner I saw," Hal remembered, "was Zane, as he skidded to a halt and reared right at the water's edge. I thought to myself as I watched him look out across the raging stream, 'Well, he doesn't have to worry about the bank anyway.'"

"He was very brave," said Giraffe. "He stood still beside the creek for a moment, and then, after spinning around a time or two the way zebras do, he plunged. He was able to keep his head above the water well enough, but the current swept him downstream until he was lost to our sight behind a grove of alders. Zebras are not really made for swimming."

"We didn't have much time to worry about Zane, however," Hal said, taking up the story, "before Lucy appeared. She didn't hesitate although she must have heard Leo roar above the storm and warn her to stop; but she jumped right in, hooves down, didn't she, Giraffe?"

"Yes," Giraffe agreed, "all the competitors were brave, even Kanga, who was actually braver than she should have been."

"But the next ones to appear," Hal said, "were Rudolph, Peter, and Bo Bo, who followed one another in closer order than I had expected. And each one, after pausing for a deep breath, followed Zane and Lucy into the raging water. They were caught in the current and swept out of sight, let me tell you, almost before we recognized them: it really was The Great Missouri Creek that day, wasn't it Casper?"

"Yes, owing to the courtesy of nature, it had become a crocodile's race course."

"But before you showed up, Casper," said Giraffe, "Gloria and Kanga, who had been hopping along together, came on the scene. By then the storm had passed, the rain was almost over, and the sun, which was emerging, made the creek glitter. We watched Gloria with great excitement: she obviously understood she would have to wade in to reach the alders she had planned to traverse. But after stopping a moment to scratch her head, she stepped right in. The water was much too wild and much too deep for wading, however, and, whether she wanted to or not, Gloria had to swim. The funny thing is, after avoiding the water for weeks, she found, like Lucy before her, she loved it. I wish it had gone the same way with Kanga."

"I was watching Dr. Oscar the orangutan, Gloria's coach," Hal recalled. "He was standing bareheaded down by the water, stationed at the motorboat beside Fergus the footman's son. When he realized what his pupil was thinking, he yelled across the creek, 'No, Gloria, no, don't go in the water: you won't be able to reach the alders; it's too deep.' But when he saw her begin to swim—and she had a beautiful overhand stroke, let me tell you—he changed his tune: 'Gloria, Gloria, look at you; keep swimming; don't go to the alders! Keep swimming and you'll win the race! Look at her go, Fergus, look at her go. We don't have to rescue Gloria, Gloria, the Olympian.'"

"And it was true," Giraffe agreed, "but that wasn't the case with Kanga. She was terrified of the water, as we could tell—she always had been—and she stood beside it without moving for several seconds until she saw her running partner, Gloria, swimming along, as Dr. Oscar's shouts made clear, toward Olympic gold. That was too much. She dropped back a little way, as she had done in practice, took a few big hops and launched herself, Roo and herself, out over the stream.

"Luckily, Fergus was ready. He had started the motor on his boat when Zane plunged into the creek; and he very nearly set out after Bo Bo, who seemed to have trouble at first righting himself; but he judged that Rudolph, Peter, and Bo Bo, all three, no matter how far the stream carried them, would be able to swim along. Fergus studied at Harvard, you know, Allison. But Kanga's situation, as he understood immediately, was another matter. 'Jump in the boat, Dr. Oscar,' he cried, 'jump in: Kanga needs help. Gloria's fine, but Kanga can't swim!'

"And with the doctor still climbing in, he launched out into the torrent to rescue Kanga—just in time.

"She was able to keep her own head above the water although she had already swallowed quite a lot, but her pouch was fully submerged, and she couldn't turn over to expose it to the air. She was trying to, but keeping herself afloat was almost more than she could do. In fact, despite flailing with her arms and legs and tail, Kanga herself was sinking when Fergus pulled up beside her.

"'Haul her in, doctor, haul her in before she sinks,'

he shouted. And it was all Dr. Oscar could do, even with his powerful arms, to drag Kanga out of the creek and into Fergus's boat. Once he had her secure, Dr. Oscar, who knew like everyone else that Roo would be in Kanga's pouch, reached down in and extracted the breathless child. Needless to say Kanga's pouch was brimming. 'Oh, Roo,' she cried as Dr. Oscar brought him out, 'oh, Roo, why did I make you come with me? Why didn't I leave you at home with a sitter? Or safe on shore at the cotton candy stand? Oh, Roo, wake up, wake up, and I'll let you have all the cotton candy you want!'

"Dr. Oscar gave Roo mouth-to-mouth resuscitation, patting his back and squeezing his belly at the same time; and finally Roo vomited up the water he had swallowed in his mother's flooded pouch and began to cry. 'Good,' said Dr. Oscar, 'good: Roo will be fine now—but no cotton candy, Kanga, and not even a glass of mead until I say so.'"

Casper took up the story. "I had just scrambled to the edge of what used to be the bank of the creek, having managed my tail all the way across the meadow as I had planned to do, when I saw Dr. Oscar hauling Kanga and Roo into Fergus's boat. The crowd in the stands seemed to be almost exploding with excitement. The only other contestants I could see as I shook my head and tried to get my bearings were Lucy and Gloria, both of whom had obviously been swept way downstream. Each of them was making good headway, however, and I saw with surprise how strongly Gloria with those great arms of hers was swimming along; but I didn't have time to think about anything but my own way of getting across the swift, glittering stream.

"Unlike the meadow, Giraffe, it presented a challenge for which, even with a tired tail, I was well-equipped."

"Oh, yes," Allison exclaimed, "I can almost see you, Casper, as you surveyed The Great Missouri Creek."

"I aimed my nose—"

"Your swollen nose," Hal muttered with a chuckle.

"I aimed my swollen nose, Allison, upstream against the flow knowing, as I slid across the creek, the opposing current would carry and deposit me just in front of the palace gate."

"Oh Casper," said Allison, "I wish I had been there to swim along beside you."

"The slope was covered with water, Hal, so this time there were no big rocks to trouble me. And when I crawled ashore, just a few yards away from Princess Isabel at the finish line, I was clearly ahead of all my rivals.

"But the race was not over. Gloria, who had climbed to shore a hundred yards or so downstream, was hopping up the bank toward me. Further downstream, Lucy was about to leave the water, and I could hear Leo roaring encouragement to her above the boisterous cheers of the crowd. I knew she would eat up the distance to the gate with wonderful leaps once she shook off the water.

"As I watched Gloria come hopping toward the gate,

I tucked my tail beneath my hind legs and, using it as a kind of lever—as I had been practicing throughout the weeks of training—I propelled myself toward the goal. Again and yet again I heaved myself ahead, scrambling between times as fast as my legs and claws could carry me. All the while, as the cheers of the crowd grew louder, Gloria was gaining, bouncing along almost as fast, it seemed to me, as Kanga might have done if she and Roo hadn't gotten swallowed by the stream.

"But just before Gloria caught up with me, I thrust my nose through the gateway, and, as I skidded to a stop exhausted, I heard Princess Isabel proclaim: 'Casper is the victor.' At almost the same time Gloria hopped by me, and Princess Isabel proclaimed: 'Gloria is second,' and a few seconds later: 'Lucy is third.'

"Both Rudolph and Peter, although each of them had to run along the bank for more than a mile, finished the race, coming fourth and fifth—as Princess Isabel proclaimed."

"They were good Olympians," Giraffe said to Allison, "completing the course although, as they well knew, they had lost all chance for victory. Kanga and Roo, who hadn't been able to finish the race, were taken to the palace infirmary. And so was Bo Bo. Billy the beaver, who understood how perilous the creek would be for Bo Bo—lacking enough fat in his tail—had run along the bank of the creek once he saw Bo Bo plunge in; and he had caught up with him, almost drowned, a mile or so downstream: the current was wicked. Billy had jumped in and dragged Bo Bo to safety. Then he had taken him to the palace infirmary where he spent a couple days with Kanga and Roo until they were all recovered.

"Zane had struggled ashore downstream on the far side of the creek. He galloped back up the meadow when he'd recovered from his swim to find out who had won the race. 'Casper first; Gloria second; Lucy third,' I shouted across to him through my megaphone. And when he heard it, he reared in salute, whinnied his congratulations, and trotted back to his home. And that is pretty much the whole story."

"Not quite the whole story, Giraffe," said Hal with as small a smile as is possible for a hippo: "Not quite the whole story, is it, Casper?"

❄ ❄ ❄

"Everybody was sporting about Casper's victory, Allison," Giraffe insisted with some emphasis: "Peter and Rudolph both helped him mount the victory stand; and it was quite a task. Everybody was sporting."

"Not quite everybody, let me tell you, Giraffe," said Hal: "Have you forgotten the controversy at the end of the race, and the fuss Dr. Oscar the orangutan made at the finish line?"

"Tell me about it," Allison requested: "Tell me about it, Casper."

"I was lying beneath the gate, too exhausted to drag

my tail through, when I became aware of Dr. Oscar the orangutan shouting and waving his arms at Princess Isabel: 'Gloria won,' he was arguing: 'She was the first one completely through the gate. Look! Casper is still not through. His tail and his hind quarters are outside.

"'Isn't that so, Giraffe?' Dr. Oscar appealed to the Olympic president, who had just galloped up: 'Gloria hopped right through the gateway, the first person through; and, although Lucy has also finished the race, Casper still has a way to go. Look at him: he may not even get the bronze, unless he puts a move on: here comes Rudolph the raccoon for third.'

"'The first competitor to break the plane is the winner,' Princess Isabel asserted: 'and as I judged the finish, Casper first broke the plane—with his nose. He is the winner.'

"'Is that fair, Giraffe?' Dr. Oscar asked. 'Casper put the first nose through the plane, as the princess calls it, but Gloria was the first person through.' He argued pretty hard at you, didn't he, Giraffe?"

"Yes, he did," Giraffe, acknowledged: "He was Gloria's coach, you must remember, Allison, and he had just seen her swim the creek—something he had never imagined she was capable of: he was very proud of her."

"But Casper won the race, didn't he?" Allison asked anxiously: "His nose broke the plane—and after such a heroic effort!"

"Yes, Casper won: Princess Isabel never wavered in her judgment; and I supported her completely, didn't I, Hal, despite my recognizing some merit in Dr. Oscar's argument?"

"Giraffe and the princess both stood firm, Allison, let me tell you, and, fortunately, Gloria, who was elated with her own performance—and her surprising new achievement—supported them very generously. 'Dr. Oscar,' she said, 'the rules are the rules: Casper broke the plane: he won and he deserved to win. Besides, it's not winning but competing that matters, isn't it, Giraffe? And I am so happy to get the silver medal, I could never begrudge Casper the gold.' Then she went over to Casper, who was just beginning to recover from his effort, and shook his claw."

"Yes," Casper said, "almost the first thing I remember clearly is Gloria's congratulations; she was very sporting, true to the principle of the Olympics Giraffe had so often explained to us. Lucy also congratulated me, and then Rudolph and Peter helped me mount the victor's stand. All the people except for Dr. Oscar cheered and cheered as I took the highest place; and then Giraffe hung the medals around our necks."

"Of course," Hal said, "Giraffe couldn't get the ribbon that your medal was attached to all the way down, could he, Casper?"

"Far enough, far enough down," Giraffe interrupted, "and when Casper raised his nose, the gold glittered in the afternoon sunlight."

"Oh," Allison exclaimed, "I wish I could have seen it."

"Actually," Hal responded, "I thought you might have such a wish, so I hid Casper's gold in Giraffe's green-leafy salad, and if he'll work his tongue down beneath the remaining leaves, I believe he will find it."

In a few seconds, indeed, Giraffe wrapped his tongue around Casper's medal; he produced it with a flourish; and, almost as formally as he had done at the Olympics, he hung it on the champion, snugly fitting the ribbon all the way down Casper's fine long nose so it shone at his throat.

"Oh," Allison cried, "it's beautiful, Casper, beautiful."

Finding a Tree

❄ ❄ ❄

It took a good shake, a good shaking,
by his friend, Rudolph the raccoon,
to wake Giraffe from a bad dream that
had made him tremble and groan.

Rudolph, who had trudged over to Giraffe's cave through the first snow of winter to light a fire for his African friend, found him shivering in his sleep and moaning, "That's no tree, it's just a twig!"

Rudolph immediately roused him. "Giraffe, Giraffe, what's the matter? Wake up; you're having a nightmare."

When Giraffe rubbed a hoof over his eyes and began to come around, Rudolph said, "Tell me what's wrong: what were you dreaming about? Were you cold?"

"No," Giraffe answered sleepily. "I wasn't cold, although I was uncomfortable, and I have a little crick in my neck."

"Too bad," his friend responded; but he was more curious than sympathetic—that Rudolph—and he went on, "Tell me about your dream, Giraffe; tell me quick before you forget it."

"I dreamed you and Peter o'Possum and the two beavers, Billy and Bo Bo, were dragging a spruce tree into my cave," Giraffe began sleepily. "It was beautiful and savory, but much too big. You were able to force it down the tunnel here into my living room, but after you got it in, you had to leave it on its side. Even so, there was no room for anyone: Peter had to cling to a branch; the rest of you were so tangled in prickles you could hardly move; and I had to bend my head around the trunk so I got a crick in my neck." And when Giraffe tried to straighten up, he gave a little cry.

"Yes?" Rudolph said, as Giraffe paused to let the pain subside. "Go on, go on; what next?"

"Well," Giraffe went on, "we agreed the tree was too big and we'd have to trim it, that is, we'd have to cut it way down. Billy and Bo Bo went right to work, chewing; and this is strange, but each branch, as they chewed it off, vanished from sight. You and Peter and I gave instructions: 'Chew here, Billy, and take this branch, Bo Bo.' Little by little, we brought the tree down to size."

"And every branch vanished as it was chewed off?" Rudolph asked.

"That's right," Giraffe said, as he gave his neck a little twitch. "All that was left when Billy and Bo Bo were finished was a twig, a miserable twig; and there wasn't any Christmas spirit left in it."

"You did have a nightmare," Rudolph sighed. "No Christmas spirit." And he wagged his head from side to side.

"But don't you see, Rudolph," Giraffe exclaimed, "it wasn't a nightmare: it was the truth. That is the way things are. My cave is too small for anything but a twig; it's too small for Christmas!" He gave his head a careful stretch and repeated disconsolately, "It's too small for Christmas." The two friends stared around Giraffe's cave in dismay.

It was a very pleasant room. The moss floor was soft; the rock walls were solid; the rock ceiling was high enough for Giraffe to sit at ease, if not high enough for him to stand. He had all the shelves and hooks and drawers he needed; and there was enough honey and enough bark and enough dry fodder stacked in one corner and more than enough bananas hanging in another to make him comfortable all winter. But it wasn't big enough for Christmas.

After a pause, Rudolph said, "What about your deck?" and the two friends crawled through the tunnel and looked around outside to see if that would do.

It was a very nice deck. Peter o'Possum and Rudolph had spent all summer laying the stones Zane and Zack the zebras had hauled over from the old quarry; and Rudolph, who understood such things, had built a fireplace so Giraffe could entertain his friends inside or out almost all year round. But only a few friends at a time, as they both became aware. If Hal the hippo sat on one side of the fireplace, for example, and if Casper the crocodile and Allison the alligator curled up on the other, there was barely enough room for Giraffe to fetch the wassail and to balance himself on the deck's front lip. And the sides were steep. If the citizens of Montana erected any size evergreen at all, there would be no room for people or for presents.

"What can we do?" Rudolph asked his friend.

"We must call a meeting," Giraffe replied, "and we must call it at once. Christmas is coming."

"Yes, a meeting," Rudolph agreed.

"But first," Giraffe suggested, "let's have a little breakfast."

Giraffe brought out a bowl of nuts and honey for Rudolph and a bowl of bark gruel for himself, and the two friends settled on opposite sides of the fire. But when Giraffe bent down to take his breakfast, his neck pinched him and he had to stand on one side of the deck and stoop all the way over to the other to reach his food.

Rudolph laughed as he watched his friend arrange

himself and said, "Well, Giraffe, you've proved your deck is not big enough for Christmas."

❄ ❄ ❄

"Where can we hold our meeting?" Rudolph asked, after the friends had had a chance to digest their food and enjoy the fire. "Where can we ask all the residents of Montana to assemble?"

"What about the palace?" Giraffe said. "I'm sure the king will allow us to use the great hall. It will be convenient for Princess Isabel and Isabel and, of course, for their majesties—if their duties allow them to attend."

"I don't think that's such a good idea," Rudolph replied. "It's too far from the pond for Casper the crocodile and Allison the alligator, for one thing; for another, I happen to know Ella the elephant feels constricted and uncomfortable there. It may seem really great to you and me, Giraffe, but it's like a closet to her."

Giraffe, who shared a love of the meadow with Ella, understood her feelings. He had always been able to creep easily through the main door of the great hall, but Ella? That was another matter. "What about the meadow?" he suggested.

"No," said Rudolph, "the beavers are nervous in the meadow, and so am I, if you want to know. But the point is, it's even further from the pond than the palace is."

"We'll never find a place," Giraffe complained, "if you're so negative."

"I wish we had a regular meeting place," Rudolph murmured almost to himself, "a big octagonal room—like the great Octagon Room at Bath, perhaps, but with big doors on every side and plenty of access to the air."

"I don't believe the Octagon Room will do us any good just now, Rudolph," Giraffe said severely. But suddenly he had a notion about a community project for next spring. Right now, however, they needed any kind of place where they could all meet, a centrally-located spot where everyone would feel safe and easy.

Rudolph seemed about to make another suggestion when Peter o'Possum came waddling through the early snow to pay Giraffe a visit. He had brought a basket of mixed leaves and, because he expected to find Rudolph at the cave, a little bag of nuts. Despite his nagging jealousy of Princess Isabel, Peter was a very generous and personable possum. The two friends were especially glad to see him because they had been on the verge of a spat and were pleased to be interrupted before it could get started.

They explained all their problems to Peter and asked for his help.

"It's true," Peter agreed, "Giraffe's cave is too small and cramped for our Christmas party; and his deck, although perfectly convenient for the three of us, is also too small: our society has grown so much recently with the addition of Gloria the gorilla and Leo the lion and now Allison the alligator. I expect Balleau the bear, although he's been off in the woods making a movie all fall, will show up as well."

"True," said Giraffe, "and we can always hope to see our friend, Rudolf the red-nosed reindeer. So what are we to do?"

"I don't have a suggestion about the tree," Peter replied, "but I do know a place where all the residents of Montana might meet to discuss the matter: the yard below my house."

"Is it close enough to the pond so Allison and Casper can scramble over?" asked Giraffe.

"And does it have enough head room for Ella?" asked Rudolph.

"Yes," answered Peter. "I've entertained all those folks recently, Ella just last night: you should have seen my kids jump off the lowest branches of our house onto her back. She's so patient with my little ones, and they can be pretty pesky."

"But is your yard roomy enough for all of us?" asked Giraffe.

"And is it smooth enough?" echoed Rudolph. "That's the point."

"You are both forgetting how many levels my house has and how grand it is. Of course, Giraffe, I could hardly expect you to climb up for a tour." Peter and Rudolph both got a laugh from the image of Giraffe wrapping his legs about the great trunk of Peter's pine and climbing up even to the lowest branches.

"The litter of needles over the years has made my yard smooth and cushiony," Peter continued, "and, if you will remember, it stretches quite a way into the woods all around. I think all the folks of the forest and the meadow will be comfortable there."

"But what about snow?" Rudolph objected. "More than a few inches would be pretty inconvenient for some of us. Think of Casper and Allison—and Roo—and me."

"It's early enough," Peter answered, "so there shouldn't be very much snow; and the beavers, with those broad tails of theirs, could brush it away in a jiffy, if there were any need. Isn't that so, Giraffe?"

"I believe you're right, Peter," said Giraffe, "now you remind me: what do you think, Rudolph?"

"It is a pleasant spot," Rudolph acknowledged, "protected but not oppressive—that's the point—and central enough so every one can attend. The beavers shouldn't feel exposed, do you think, Giraffe?"

"No," he agreed, "and Zane and Zack should not have any trouble with undergrowth."

So it was determined. And the three friends set off, each in a different direction, to summon all the residents of Montana to the house of Peter o'Possum.

❄ ❄ ❄

Giraffe, who went first to the palace, told Oscar the footman and Catherine the cook about the meeting in the yard beneath Peter o'Possum's house and asked Oscar if he might have a brief audience with the king.

"The king is in his counting house counting out his

money," Oscar reported, "and with January the first just around the corner, he is very busy. But I'll announce you," he said, before Giraffe could interrupt, "and see if he can spare you a minute. I recognize your business is important."

"And urgent, as well," Giraffe insisted. "Christmas comes before January."

"True," Oscar admitted. "I'll bring that to his majesty's attention."

The king was happy to see Giraffe. For one thing, it gave him an excuse to take a rest from his counting. Money was not very important in Montana. The residents were so solicitous of one another and so generous that money almost never changed hands. Dr. Oscar the orangutan did not charge for his services; Gloria the gorilla gave away all her banana products; and Billy the beaver had free access to the Montana woods both for food and fuel. But the money had to be counted anyway. And it was the king's job to count it.

Giraffe found him in the chilly, drab counting house, working away. He had different denominations of bills and different values of coins piled on a big table all around him. He needed the gloves he was wearing, as Giraffe noted with sympathy, but they made him very clumsy in handling the money. He seemed always to be miscounting, moreover, and having to start over again.

"The bills are the worst," he complained, "especially these old crumpled ones: they drift across the border from Wyoming and the Dakotas. Those people must waste a lot of their time in commerce. Look at this twenty, Giraffe, just look at it: it's almost torn in two. But it has to be counted just like all the rest."

Princess Isabel was helping her father, Giraffe noted with satisfaction.

"Yes," the king commented, puffing out a great wreath of warm moist air, "she's beginning to assume her royal duties. And she's almost as good at counting as I am, almost as good, or she would be if her hands didn't get so cold."

Giraffe couldn't help noticing she was in fact, even with her cold hands, a good deal better at counting than the king, who confused twenties with fifties sometimes and often dropped bills and stacks of bills on the floor.

"She will be a better monarch than her father," he thought to himself.

"I am here today," Giraffe announced with some solemnity, "on a very important matter: the community Christmas tree."

"Yes, yes," the king responded, "very important, very important. But what is the problem? We have plenty of trees to choose from here in Montana," he proclaimed with some pride. "We have spruce and cedar and fir and pine."

"True, your majesty," Giraffe agreed, "we should have no trouble in finding a tree."

"Well then," the king said, "what's the trouble? Surely no one is objecting to our having a Christmas tree."

"No, your majesty, I believe all your subjects are in favor of a tree."

"Good, good. Then let's have a tree. I'm sure her majesty and ourself approve the idea. Princess Isabel, my dear, you would like a tree, wouldn't you?"

"Yes, daddy," the princess said, "but that's not the question, is it, Giraffe?"

"No," Giraffe acknowledged, "the princess is right. The question is this: where can we erect a big enough tree on a place that will be roomy enough to allow the comfortable assembly of all your majesty's subjects? I had hoped to offer my cave, but as Rudolph the raccoon and I discovered, my cave is much too small even for a tiny tree; and my deck, although quite pleasant for small celebrations, as Princess Isabel may attest, is also too small for this occasion."

"What do you propose then, Giraffe?" asked the king. "Out with it; out with it; I don't have all day."

"I don't have a proposal, your majesty," Giraffe admitted.

"Well then," the king said somewhat huffily, "why are you wasting my time? You see all the money I still have to count, and, although you may not have noticed it, Giraffe, January the first follows soon after Christmas, soon after, and I must have all my accounts ready by then."

"I understand, your majesty, and I apologize for taking up your time. But I have come to request your attendance at a meeting of all your subjects, a meeting to determine where we may erect our Christmas tree."

"Oh," said the king, "I see, I see. That is a matter of some weight. Well then, tell me about this meeting."

"Oh, yes, Giraffe," Princess Isabel exclaimed, "tell us when and where the meeting will be held. We must have a nice Christmas, mustn't we, daddy?"

"True, true, my dear," the king replied in a kinder tone. "Tell us, Giraffe."

"The meeting to discuss the community Christmas tree," Giraffe informed them, "will be held at three o'clock this afternoon in the yard directly beneath the house of Peter o'Possum, and it is hoped all the residents of Montana will attend."

"That sounds like an excellent place," said the king, "an excellent place, and I wish I could be there; but, as you can see, Giraffe, I'm surrounded with work. I'll be lucky if I can attend the celebration."

"Daddy," Princess Isabel exclaimed, "you promised, if I counted the dimes and pennies, you'd come to Christmas."

"Yes, yes, my dear," the king responded with a sigh, "and so I shall if I can just make these bills behave." As he said this, he accidentally knocked a few to the floor.

"He doesn't really have the dexterity to be a king," Giraffe thought to himself, "or the arithmetic." He picked up a couple of bills with his tongue and tried with the tuft of his tail to straighten up a pile of twenties. "Of course," he recognized—still to himself, "I'm not cut out to be a king either."

"Our daughter, Princess Isabel of Montana, will attend the meeting in our place," the king proclaimed, "with full powers to represent our judgment. And," he went on, as if he read the question on Giraffe's face, "my other daughter, Isabel, who is suffering from the flu, and her majesty the queen, who is eating bread and honey in the parlor just now, will remain in the palace. We hope and plan, however," he concluded with a glance at the princess, "we will all be able to attend the Christmas celebration."

"We will be honored to be joined on this occasion by the princess," Giraffe responded, "even if she must come alone."

"The queen is almost as busy as ourself," the king explained, "getting through all that bread and honey is no small matter. And our laundry maid, Marian, doesn't help: she keeps interrupting her majesty with questions about the light and dark wash; you'd think, Giraffe, you'd think she didn't have any eyes."

"She is just beginning this job," said Princess Isabel.

"Yes, yes, my dear," the king admitted, "but do you think her eyes will improve with time?" He laughed heartily at his little joke.

"The queen's gracious attention and her mild speech," Giraffe said, "might have moderated our discussion, and—"

But before he could continue, all three of them heard a loud, angry voice, the queen's, ringing out from the parlor: "When you finally hang out those clothes, my girl, I hope a blackbird comes along and nips off your nose."

"Of course," the king said to Giraffe almost in a whisper, "of course, she didn't really mean it. But that girl is aggravating." When Giraffe failed to respond, he went on more loudly, "You can see, at any rate, the queen and I are too busy to attend the meeting. But Princess Isabel will represent us, and you know, Giraffe, Christmas and the Christmas tree are as important to her, quite as important, as to ourself."

With this observation, as Giraffe realized, his audience with the king had come to an end.

❄ ❄ ❄

Giraffe's next destination was the meadow, where he hoped to find both the zebras, Zane and Zack, and Ella the elephant. Peter o'Possum had offered to visit Kanga and Roo and to ask them to carry news of the meeting on to the lions before he himself went home to make everything ready. Rudolph the raccoon had promised to round up the beavers, who were needed to brush off the inch or two of new snow that had fallen since breakfast; and then he planned to go on to the pond.

Giraffe found Zane and Zack near a bracken patch in the meadow, standing head to tail as they always did in cold weather and chewing away on the last of the year's big burdock leaves, a food they both seemed, to Giraffe's amazement, to relish. "There's no accounting for tastes," he thought, as he watched them swallow the large tough leaves.

"Good morning, my dear friends," he said as he galloped up to them. "I have an important message for you."

"Okay, Giraffe," they said at once, "but first join us for the last of the burdock: it's delicious."

"Thank you," he replied and nibbled enthusiastically on a particularly resistant bit of fiber.

After he got it down and had cleared his throat, Giraffe told his friends about the problem of the Christmas tree, about the meeting to solve this problem, and about the easy route to Peter o'Possum's house. "You see, Zane," he said to the zebra with a black stripe over one eye, "all the residents of Montana are concerned in this affair."

"Yes," the zebra responded, "but I'm Zack."

"Of course," Giraffe replied, noticing too late that the other zebra, Zane, had white stripes over both his eyes. "Please excuse me; I'm so worried about the tree and our Christmas party I can't see straight."

Suddenly he knew the present he was going to give Zane and Zack for Christmas.

"I surely hope both of you come to the meeting," he said. "Remember, it's at three o'clock this afternoon."

Although they had been a little hurt that Giraffe got them confused with one another, they both assured him they would attend the meeting.

"And the party, too," Giraffe insisted.

"And the party, too," they both promised.

Giraffe said goodbye and, with a little swish of his tail, he went on across the meadow to find Ella the elephant. "She should be easy to find," he murmured to himself, "she's the biggest elephant in Montana except for herself." While he was enjoying his little joke, sure enough he recognized the impressive silhouette of his friend, emerging from a clump of willows along a tiny stream. She had a bunch of leaves in her trunk, almost the last leaves left on those trees. They looked tasty to Giraffe, but even after Ella had caught sight of him, she went on eating. "Well," he thought, "I have enough for myself stored in my cave at home, and Ella must hunt all winter for the food she needs."

"Good morning, Ella, my friend," he greeted her cheerfully, "that looks like a tasty bunch of leaves you've got in your trunk."

"Yes," Ella replied, "but it's just about the last for this season. From now on, I'll really have to search for my food."

"If you don't have any luck," Giraffe said, "you must pay me a visit: I have a good stock of fodder of one kind and another stored in my cave, and you are always welcome. You don't happen to fancy bananas, do you?"

"Thank you, Giraffe, I do like a banana now and then, actually, although what I really need is a supply of summer greenery. As it is, I choke down evergreen leaves, cedar mostly. I really hate spruce needles although Rudolph the raccoon insists they are full of nourishment. It's no fun to get one of those stuck in your trunk, Giraffe, as you may remember. Winter in Montana," Ella concluded, "is very hard for an elephant."

As she spoke, an image out of the current Sears catalog rose in Giraffe's mind, and he realized the trunk muffler Gloria the gorilla had been weaving as a gift for Ella would have to be saved for another Christmas. That reminded him of his errand.

"The citizens of Montana, Ella, are going to hold a meeting this afternoon at three o'clock in the yard at Peter o'Possum's house to discuss our Christmas tree. The problem is this: erecting a big enough tree in a roomy enough place. My cave and my deck, as Rudolph the raccoon and I came to recognize this morning, are much too small. And even the great hall of the palace, although it might be big enough, is too far from the pond to be convenient for Allison the alligator and Casper the crocodile. So you can see, we've got a problem."

"I'll be glad to attend the meeting," Ella replied, "and I think I've got some good ideas."

"Fine," Giraffe responded, "if we share our ideas together, I'm sure we'll reach a decision agreeable to us all."

"I could come over early, if you like, Giraffe, and tramp down this new snow. I'm beginning to believe, however, as I consider, it might be better just to brush it away. Stamped snow is pretty cold under foot; and it can turn to ice very quickly. What do you think?"

"I'm no more comfortable on ice than you are, Ella," he answered, "but don't worry: Rudolph the raccoon has gone over to ask the beavers to come early and sweep the ground clean. I'm sure they'll agree. Bo Bo the beaver, who is a stickler for neatness, will no doubt assemble and direct them."

"I hope Peter o'Possum controls his little ones," Ella said. "The last time I visited him and his family, they kept jumping down on my back from higher and higher branches; and they do have sharp little claws—although not like Allison the alligator or Casper the crocodile, I'm glad to say." And she raised her trunk to trumpet her amusement. "I couldn't complain," Ella went on, "because Peter had prepared such a generous green salad for me with a nice side dish of peanuts: Billy the beaver must have brought those all the way from Georgia."

"I dare say," Giraffe assured her, "the little possums will be very quiet this afternoon. Peter understands as well as you and I, we must all concentrate on the tree."

After he said goodbye to Ella, Giraffe galloped away at a pretty good clip. He had a long way to go, across the meadow and all the way up the northern path, to reach the sturdy piano box in which Gloria the gorilla maintained her residence.

❄ ❄ ❄

While Giraffe was on this journey, Peter o'Possum paid a visit to the home of Kanga and Roo. Kanga welcomed Peter into her burrow and, when he got settled, served him a hot mug of mead.

"Roo and I make it from honey, don't we, Roo?" she said with satisfaction. "How do you like it, Peter?"

It was in fact very savory and good, as Peter said, and he gratefully accepted a second mugful. Hot mead, he began to feel, was the perfect drink for the Montana winter.

"You know, Kanga," Peter said, "the recipe for this beverage would make an excellent Christmas gift for her majesty the queen. It would give some variety to her duties and aid her in getting through them."

Finding Christmas gifts for one another, as you may

have noticed, was one of the main concerns of the residents of Montana, and Peter's suggestion made Kanga very excited.

"Do you really think so, Peter?" she asked. "Do you think the queen would enjoy our mead?"

"It's a wonderful drink," Peter assured her, "especially appropriate to the queen, for whom honey is a chief concern."

"We'll be glad," Kanga exclaimed, "to share our mead with the queen, won't we, Roo?"

"The reason I have visited you today, Kanga," Peter said, after he finished his second mug of mead, "is to announce an important community gathering, a meeting to discuss our Christmas tree."

"Roo and I are very interested in the tree, aren't we, Roo?" Kanga said. "Where will it be erected this year?"

"That's the question," Peter answered. "We need a big tree raised in a large, level place to accommodate all our residents."

"Yes," said Kanga, "I see. With so many recent arrivals, and such big ones—Gloria and Allison and Leo with his pride and, of course, our special friend, Balleau, if he can spare us time—we must find a big space."

"Exactly," said Peter o'Possum. "The meeting," he went on without giving Kanga a chance to interrupt, "will be held this afternoon at three o'clock in the yard at my house, which, as Giraffe and Rudolph the raccoon and I agree, is the best place for it."

"Of course," Kanga said, "that is a perfect place for us all to meet. I hope Rudolf the red-nosed reindeer will be able to join us—although I know how busy he is at this time of the year."

"We've sent him an e-mail," Peter assured her, "but we haven't yet had a reply."

"Well, anyway," Kanga said, "Roo and I will be sure to attend, won't we Roo? You can count on us."

"Thank you, Kanga," Peter said, "but I also have another request."

"Another request; another request of Roo and me?" Kanga exclaimed. "Please tell us about it. We will be happy, more than happy, to do anything we can, won't we, Roo?"

"Giraffe has gone into the meadow to announce the meeting to Zane and Zack the zebras and to Ella the elephant; Rudolph is telling the beavers and the inhabitants of the pond. We hope you and Roo will carry the tidings over to the lions. I believe Roo plays sometimes with their little ones."

"That's true," Kanga acknowledged, "our families are on close terms, and Roo is especially fond of Larry the lion. Larry's a little rough sometimes, isn't he, Roo? But they usually get along. It's wonderful to see Roo riding on Larry's back, playing cowboy."

"I'm sure it's a sight," Peter said. "Do you think you might visit them right now, and tell them about the meeting?"

"I'll be happy to and so will Roo. It's pretty chilly, of course, and you won't be as cozy in my pouch as I could hope, will you, Roo? But this is such an important errand—such an honor to be trusted like this—we will pay no attention to the weather, will we, Roo? I'll wrap you up in my shawl and fasten on your earmuffs, and we will hop right over to the lions with our message."

"Thank you," said Peter o'Possum as he made a note to himself about Christmas presents for Kanga and Roo. "Thank you very much."

"I do wish Roo could be a little cozier in my pouch," Kanga whispered to Peter as he rose to leave, "but I'll just put some of this hot mead in a bottle for him and I'm sure he'll be fine. Good bye, Peter, good bye. Such a good friend, isn't he, Roo, such a good friend."

❄ ❄ ❄

Rudolph the raccoon did not find Billy the beaver at home when he arrived at the beavers' dam, but that did not surprise him. Luckily, Bo Bo was around, and he was eager to help. The snow had got deeper than Giraffe or Peter expected, deeper than usual for the time of year in Montana. But Bo Bo assured Rudolph he would assemble a troop of beavers, and they would brush Peter's yard clean right down to the needles before three o'clock.

"We all feel honored to serve the folks of Montana," Bo Bo announced. "Besides, we love to exercise our tails making things neat and clean. We will also be happy to use our teeth," he continued, "when the time comes to chop the tree you and Giraffe and all our friends choose for the community Christmas."

"Bo Bo was a very accommodating beaver," Rudolph

thought to himself, "but he was a little bit ostentatious. The lack of fat in his tail probably had something to do with it," Rudolph supposed, and he decided to take this up with Giraffe, "who," as Rudolph admitted to himself, "understands such things better than I do."

He thanked Bo Bo, confident the beavers would carry out their task—"That was the point about Bo Bo," Rudolph realized—and made his way to the pond, hoping it hadn't frozen over yet.

It hadn't, although it was beginning to get near the freezing point, and a steamy mist was rising from it. The first person Rudolph saw through the mist was Hal the hippo, who was, as Rudolph gradually realized, exercising vigorously on the bank.

"Getting ready for your trek to the coast?" Rudolph inquired.

"Yes," Hal replied, "it's a very demanding trip: the stream I must follow has some pretty fierce rapids; and once out of the mountains, it curves and curves. All in all, let me tell you, Rudolph, I face a tough journey."

"If you went overland the last part," Rudolph suggested, "you could make it a lot shorter. And you are a great deal more agile on land, Hal, than one might suppose."

"That's true," Hal agreed readily, "I am really quite agile, but the truth is, Rudolph, I don't have any sense of direction. The stream leads me right to the home of my relatives, Herbert and Hannah the hippos, but if I leave it, I'll be sure to get lost. And Oregon, let me tell you, is no place for a hippo to get lost."

"In that case," Rudolph agreed, "you'd better stick to the stream." But while he was saying this, he was deciding on a perfect Christmas present for his friend.

"I'm visiting you today, Hal, on a special errand. Peter o'Possum, Giraffe, and I are calling a meeting of all the citizens of Montana to discuss the community Christmas tree."

"A good idea," said Hal. "I've been wondering about it myself. Where can we find a place big enough, smooth enough, and convenient enough for all our friends? I was asking myself this question just the other day. Giraffe's cave is central, of course, and an easy walk for Allison the alligator and Casper the crocodile—and that's a matter of some importance, Rudolph, let me tell you. But it's too small, much too small: there's Ella the elephant for one thing."

"Yes, yes," Rudolph interrupted with some impatience, "we've thought of these things, Hal, and that's why we're calling a meeting."

"Splendid," Hal responded, "but it must be held in a place everyone will find convenient. There's the great hall in the palace, of course, if Ella won't find it uncomfortable, but it may be too far from the pond."

"Yes, yes," Rudolph once again interrupted his friend. "That's why we've decided to hold the meeting in the yard beneath Peter o'Possum's house."

"Good choice," Hal said while Rudolph paused for a breath. "Peter's place should be close enough for Casper and Allison and roomy enough for Ella. But what about snow, Rudolph? Have you thought about snow?"

"Yes, Hal, we've thought of that, too. Bo Bo and

the beavers are going to brush all the snow away so even the small folks will be comfortable. Now then, will you join us? The meeting is scheduled for three o'clock today."

"Of course, I'll attend," Hal answered cheerfully. "Three-thirty today. But I hope you plan to ask Casper the crocodile and Allison the alligator, too. Let me tell you, they are as interested in Christmas as anybody."

"Of course, Hal, everyone is invited. I was hoping to run into them now, or, if not, to ask you to inform them."

"That won't be necessary," Hal said, "here they come." And indeed Rudolph could see Allison's white snub nose and Casper's elegant brown proboscis, sliding toward them through the still pond water.

Before he could greet them, however, Hal called out, "Here's our friend Rudolph the raccoon come to invite us to an important meeting in the yard at Peter o'Possum's house to discuss our Christmas tree; we're meeting there at three-thirty today."

"Yes," Rudolph agreed with a revision, "at three o'clock today. I hope you can make it."

"We're all expected to attend," Hal chimed in.

"Yes," Rudolph agreed again, although he was a little put out at Hal's eagerness. "We must decide on a place that will be large enough and level enough and accessible enough to accommodate all the residents of Montana."

"Allison and I will be happy to attend the meeting," Casper said, but before Allison could agree, she spied a trout, her favorite Montana fish, swimming up to the surface and slid back into the pond.

"Actually," Casper explained, "she's still shy of us. What's more, she's a little homesick. She especially misses her old cypress log."

"What about a nice pine or spruce log?" Rudolph suggested. "I'm sure Bo Bo the beaver would chew down any tree you chose; and Ella the elephant or Zane and Zack the zebras would help you drag it into place—right beside your patio, perhaps."

"Thank you, Rudolph," Casper replied."I've thought about pine; I even mentioned it to Allison. But for her, it's the old cypress log from her home in Florida or nothing. She says having her log would make her feel really at home here."

"I don't know," Rudolph admitted, and it was an admission he hated to make. "Getting a big log up here from Florida? I'm not sure I know how."

"I understand, Rudolph," Casper agreed. "Hal and I have not been able to come up with anything either."

"And we've both been thinking about it," Hal added. "We're very worried about Allison, let me tell you. She's a sweet alligator and we're fond of her, but if we can't help her get over being homesick, I don't think she'll stay here in Montana."

"Especially now with winter closing in," Casper added and gnashed his teeth with worry.

"Well," Rudolph responded, "I'll think this over, myself, and I'll ask Giraffe if he has any ideas."

"Thank you, Rudolph!" Casper cried. "I'm sure Giraffe will be able to come up with something: he's so smart."

"Surely, surely," Rudolph said, although he was a little hurt that Casper and Hal—who had nodded enthusiastically as Casper spoke—should think Giraffe was any smarter than he was. "We'll put our two heads together," he assured Casper, "and I'm sure we'll come up with something.

"What about a cedar log," Rudolph said, as if he'd just had a good afterthought. "It has a wonderful scent, much better than cypress, I dare say," although, as he himself recognized, he didn't know how cypress smelled.

"No, Rudolph," Casper replied, "I'm afraid the old cypress log, whatever it smells like, is the only one that will make Allison feel at home."

"Very well, then," Rudolph promised him, "Giraffe and I will work on this problem until we solve it, have no fear."

With this assurance he left his two friends and returned to his burrow for a little nap before the meeting.

Meanwhile, Giraffe reached Gloria the gorilla's piano box. Gloria had painted it bright yellow and trimmed it with stripes of brown and green; and she had roofed it with a steep curving tip of palm leaves. It sat at the center of a grove of banana trees—the only ones in Montana. So it was easy for Giraffe to recognize.

Luckily he found not only Gloria there but her guest,

Dr. Oscar the orangutan. Dr. Oscar often swung over to visit Gloria, as everyone knew, and to share her famous banana punch. They were having a glass, actually a second glass, when Giraffe knocked.

Unfortunately, Gloria, who had enjoyed a couple of glasses before Dr. Oscar dropped in, was suffering a little bout of dyspepsia. "Oh, Giraffe," she complained, "I feel very bad—such gas pains!" And after a pause to catch her breath, she continued, "If only I had some bromo seltzer or some tums for the tummy."

"You must have something in your bag, Dr. Oscar," Giraffe suggested to her guest.

"No, I'm sorry to say," replied the doctor, scratching his head. "I have my bag here with me, of course, but there's no room in it for stomach remedies."

"Oh," Gloria groaned, "I feel so bad."

"Well then," Dr. Oscar said, "I will just swing back over to my place and fetch the medicine we need. It will only take me a minute. Would you mind staying with Gloria, Giraffe, until I get back?"

"Not at all," Giraffe responded, "I'll just begin telling Gloria about the problem that brought me over here."

"Fine," Dr. Oscar said and, without more ado, he swung himself up into the forest and away.

The second he was gone, Gloria scratched her head, shrugged and said, "I had to get Dr. Oscar out of the way for a minute, Giraffe, so I could show you the Christmas present I ordered for him."

"Then you aren't sick?" Giraffe asked.

"Sick?" Gloria answered with a laugh. "Since when can a little of my own delicious banana punch make me sick? But look here, what do you think of this?" and she produced a fine round box that contained a fancy black bowler. "Isn't it just the thing for a doctor? Everybody will be able to recognize him now."

"True," replied Giraffe, although for a moment he wanted to ask how many people in Montana had had trouble recognizing Dr. Oscar the orangutan even without such a hat.

Instead, he said, "It's a beautiful present, Gloria, and I'm sure Dr. Oscar will be very pleased. He'll wear it everywhere he goes, I bet, and when we see him we'll all say, 'Here comes Dr. Oscar the orangutan in his fine black bowler.'"

"Thank you, Giraffe, I'm so glad you approve."

She had just put the bowler back in its box and stored it out of sight when Dr. Oscar came swinging down from the trees with a little bag of stomach remedies. Gloria groaned, took an especially big pill he prescribed and, after a little while, said she felt a lot better. It was quite a performance, but as Giraffe thought about it later, he remembered Gloria had been connected to a traveling circus before she settled down to raise bananas in Montana.

"I have visited you today," he said, glad finally to get on with his errand, "to announce a meeting: all the citizens of our state are asked to come to the yard beneath the house of Peter o'Possum at three o'clock this afternoon to discuss the question of the community Christmas tree. I

104

hope," he said, lowering his voice and filling it with sympathy, "your health, Gloria, will allow you to attend. Perhaps if Dr. Oscar remains in close attendance with his bag of pills, you will be able to join us with no ill effects. What do you think, doctor?"

"I agree, Giraffe," Dr. Oscar replied while he reached up his hand carefully to his head, "especially if she avoids banana punch for the next day or two."

"Yes, by all means," Giraffe assented, "avoid banana punch."

❄ ❄ ❄

Allison the alligator and Casper the crocodile were the first to appear in Peter o'Possum's yard: they had left the pond early to make sure they arrived on time. Everything was ready for the meeting. Bo Bo and the beavers, who were as good as their word, had brushed the yard clean to the very edge and surrounded it with a little wall of sparkling new snow, leaving gateways for each of the paths. The sky above was frosty blue, but the afternoon sun made the floor of pine needles glisten. Before the beavers came, the possums had dusted the snow, not only off the cones, but off all the leafy branches of their home. So Allison and Casper, as they entered Peter's yard, found themselves in a sunny winter bower, green above and golden under foot.

"Isn't it beautiful?" exclaimed Allison, who was entranced with snow. "The perfect arena for our discussion."

She seemed, at least for the moment, to have forgotten about her old cypress log.

Everybody arrived on time except Hal the hippo, who explained he had been confused about the schedule. "Somehow I got the notion we were meeting at three-thirty; I hope I'm not too late to participate; I hate tardiness, let me tell you."

Leo and Lucy, who had left their pride at home, appeared in naked majesty, but others had adorned themselves in various festive ways. Rudolph the raccoon had donned a red-and-white stocking cap for the occasion; Ella the elephant was sporting a cedar—not spruce—wreath; and Giraffe displayed a broad green satin sash which his friends had given him last Christmas. Princess Isabel was wearing a new red cloak—"So becoming," Kanga exclaimed—and a pair of large, wool mittens. "She won't be able to count money in those," Giraffe thought with satisfaction.

Gloria the gorilla and Dr. Oscar the orangutan brought a steaming pail full of banana punch—full except for what they had drunk on the hike over. Kanga arrived with a pint of mead, hoping to try it out on Princess Isabel before she gave the queen her recipe. Oscar the footman and Fergus the footman's son came lugging a great vat of hot chocolate, which swung between them on a heavy pole. Catherine the cook, who had made it, remained at the palace, baking bread for the queen; so did Marian the maid: no one knew why. Their majesties were absent, as they had explained they would be; but they sent their greetings and apologies. Isabel also missed this important meeting although, as Princess Isabel told everyone, she had wanted to come so badly she almost climbed out of her sick bed.

Otherwise, almost all the adult residents of Montana were present except for Balleau the bear, who was stuck doing some re-takes for his latest movie, and Rudolf the red-nosed reindeer, who was presumably busy up at the north pole preparing for Christmas eve.

"I wish," Giraffe murmured to Princess Isabel, who was standing beside him at the base of Peter o'Possum's pine, "Rudolf had answered our e-mail: I would feel better knowing for sure he is aware of our assembly."

"Yes," the princess agreed, "but I think we had better start without him and hope we receive word later."

She stepped forward to address the folks who had come. "Citizens of Montana," she said, raising her voice so all could hear, "we are gathered to consider the setting and the arrangements for our Christmas celebration. As several of you have recognized, we face a number of problems. We must not only select our tree, but we must also decide where to hold our festivity so all the citizens of the state can attend with comfort, safety, and convenience. I hereby declare the meeting to consider this question to be, in the name of my father, King Cole, open for discussion."

"I wish the pond were frozen over," said Peter o'Possum to get things started. "Then we could raise the tree there."

"That's a terrible idea," answered Hal the hippo. "The pond would never be solid enough to support the larger folks, let me tell you, not at least by Christmas."

"That's right, Hal," said Ella. "And even if it were solid, it would be too slippery to be safe for everybody."

"I suppose you would like to raise our tree out in the meadow, Ella," said Rudolph the raccoon. "Some of us don't feel comfortable out there, any more than you do on ice. Besides, think of the trouble it will be for Zane and Zack—yes, and maybe for you, too—to move a big enough tree out into the meadow."

"Especially if we choose a spruce," said Zane, the zebra with white stripes over both his eyes. "They have such prickly needles."

"True," Ella agreed.

"I would be happy to entertain the celebration beneath my banana trees," said Gloria the gorilla, who had just enjoyed her fourth glass of banana punch, "but I don't have much open space."

"It's too far to your place anyway," snapped Casper the crocodile. "We shouldn't expect Allison the alligator, who is a new resident in our state, to have to scramble so far."

"What about the great hall in the palace?" suggested Oscar the footman, who was still puffing a little from carrying the hot chocolate.

"Not a bad idea," echoed Kanga, as she reached into her pouch to give Roo a little squeeze. "Then we'd be sure to be cozy no matter what the weather's like."

"True," said Dr. Oscar the orangutan, "but the hall is even further from the pond than Gloria's banana grove. It doesn't matter to me, I can swing over from tree to tree, but Allison and Casper would find it quite a scramble."

"And besides," Ella chimed in, "the great hall is too small for some of us. You have trouble just creeping in the door, don't you, Giraffe?"

"Yes," Giraffe agreed. "The great hall, which was my first choice, is inconvenient, now especially that our numbers have increased."

"I still like the idea of the pond," said Peter o'Possum, "if we're just patient enough to wait until it's well frozen. We can put rubber pads on your feet, Ella, and make you feel quite at home."

"No," Ella responded with a long snort, "I'd still worry about the ice cracking under me."

"Not only that," Hal said, "but Christmas will be long gone, let me tell you, and so will I, by the time the pond is frozen."

"And Allison and I will be frozen as stiff as the pond," said Casper, giving his tail a twitch.

"And Balleau the bear will be fast asleep in his cave," added Kanga.

"Very well, very well," Peter replied peevishly, "let somebody else make a better suggestion."

"Roo and I had always hoped we could all meet and celebrate at Giraffe's cave," Kanga said wistfully.

"Me, too," Allison agreed. "That is the middle of Montana."

"We beavers can chew down a nice tree almost any place," said Bo Bo.

"But not too far from where you want us to drag it," objected Zane and Zack together.

"Spruce trees are very savory," Gloria suggested as she scratched her back against the trunk of Peter's pine.

"Except for their needles," Ella complained.

"True," Dr. Oscar was forced to acknowledge as he reached for his head. "I remember removing spruce needles from several hands and feet . . ."

"And trunks," Ella muttered.

" . . . that we picked up from decorating the tree last Christmas," Dr. Oscar continued.

"What about a nice cedar?" cried Rudolph.

"Or a yew?" squeaked Marvin the mole, who had just popped up.

"There aren't any yew trees in Montana," Rudolph exclaimed with exasperation. A spat seemed to be brewing. Giraffe, who saw it coming, directed an appealing glance toward Leo the lion.

"Excuse me, your highness," Leo roared out, turning his fine head with deference toward Princess Isabel, "will it please you to hear me speak a word?"

"Of course, Leo," she responded, "what would you like to say?"

"It seems to me," Leo observed, pausing to growl respectfully at the back of his throat, "we have made excellent progress today except on two points: we haven't been able to select a tree; and we haven't been able to agree on where to place it." This made everyone laugh, somewhat shamefaced, and restored the Christmas spirit.

"I'm sure," Giraffe began when things quieted down a little, "we all want the same thing for our Christmas: the grandest tree erected in the most convenient place. And although this presents problems, partly because we are all different from one another—different in many ways—I still believe, if we reason together, we can solve them and organize a Christmas that will bring joy to us all."

There was a moment of silence after Giraffe finished speaking. Then suddenly everyone heard what sounded like a small clap of thunder and, right afterwards, the tinkling of bells coming from the tip top of Peter o'Possum's pine. When they turned their eyes upward into the darkening sky, they saw Rudolf the red-nosed reindeer, fully harnessed for his Christmas journey, pausing above them. As soon as he became aware of their presence below, he bent his head and began to circle. Down he swooped, tracing a shiny spiral on the air as he passed round and round Peter's tree and landing finally in front of Princess Isabel on the gleaming pine floor. All at once, Giraffe knew the right place and the right tree for the Montana Christmas.

"Greetings, your highness," Rudolf said with a bow. "Please forgive my tardiness. Things have gotten pretty busy at the North Pole. I may be able only to salute you as I pass by with Santa on Christmas eve, but I am eager to assist all my Montana friends in choosing their tree. I am always with you in spirit."

"Welcome, Rudolf," Princess Isabel replied. "Can he help us in our deliberations, Giraffe?"

"He already has, your highness: in fact, he has shown us the solution to all our problems."

"Have I?" Rudolf cried with astonishment.

"Has he, Giraffe?" echoed Peter o'Possum.

"Yes, he has," Giraffe answered, "if you have the true Christmas spirit, Peter." Turning to Rudolph the raccoon, Giraffe asked him, "You understand, don't you?"

"I believe so," Rudolph said.

"And you, Princess Isabel, you understand?"

"Yes," she responded. "Friends, citizens of Montana, we have much to do to prepare for Christmas. We must gather together to adorn our tree, to assemble our presents, and to organize our celebration. But we already know the tree we must adorn and the place where we must meet. Here is the tree," she declared, putting her hand on the great trunk of Peter o'Possum's pine, "and this is the place."

Christmas

❄ ❄ ❄

Winter in Montana, as Ella had complained to Giraffe, was hard for an elephant. She could brush or blow away the first snow easily enough, even if it was heavy, and locate the food—the scraps of turf, the dead leaves, the twigs—which allowed her to maintain herself in the cold. But after the first thaw and the freeze that followed, the earth was covered in a sheet of ice, and then the problem of finding food was almost more than she could solve. With her tusks, she gouged a little bark off the trees; and with her trunk, which Ella had used to snatch sweet grasses and bushes all through the warm months, she tore rough foliage from evergreens. She ate mostly cedar leaves, coarse as they were, and, when she lost her appetite for them, the dangerous needles of the spruce.

It wasn't Rudolph the raccoon's recommendation of spruce as nutritious that made Ella try such a food; it was the meagerness of the supply or, at least, the narrowness of her choices. When she got a needle lodged in her trunk— well, at least, it gave her an excuse to visit Dr. Oscar the orangutan and enjoy a little company. If he was over at the home of Gloria the gorilla, so much the better: the three of them might share a bucket of Gloria's famous banana punch. Ella couldn't help envying Zane and Zack, with whom she shared the meadow, when she watched them standing head to tail or, if the wind rose, huddling together in a cozy brake back in the woods. For most of the winter Ella was alone— and lonely—besides being hungry.

Almost nobody was accessible even to his closest friends in the winter time. The snow got too deep, and the cold became too intense for travel. True, Gloria the gorilla and Dr. Oscar the orangutan got together in Gloria's piano box, which Gloria had insulated with banana peels; but then,

Dr. Oscar could swing through the trees almost as well during one season as another. Neither he nor Gloria visited anyone else, except of course when somebody took sick. One winter, when Rudolph the raccoon came down with diphtheria, Dr. Oscar spent a lot of time swinging between his own home and the ice-bound stream where Rudolph had his burrow. In fact, Dr. Oscar had to swing on over to the palace that year and establish a clinic to inoculate all the citizens of Montana. Otherwise, Montanans lay low during the winter time.

Allison the alligator and Casper the crocodile stiffened and slept in the mud bank Casper had gouged out in the warm weather; Rudolph the raccoon, even when he was well, emerged from his burrow only to search for food or sniff the air for signs of spring; Peter o'Possum remained fairly active, dropping by Giraffe's cave now and then: he was a tough little fellow with a thick coat; but Kanga and Roo, when they did not make the arduous trip back to England, huddled in their nest, making do on the honey they had stored during the summer and the treats—the nuts, acorns, and bananas—infrequent visitors brought them. Giraffe, whose coat was as thin as Kanga's, also spent most of the winter indoors, hovering near his fire. All the beavers kept to their dam after Christmas; and no trains ran along the Montana line.

Hal the hippo went down the stream to Oregon and lived through the season in a temperate lake with his relatives just over the coastal range from the Pacific. But except for him and Balleau the bear, who hibernated somewhere off in a secret den in the wilderness, almost everybody stayed at home. "Our society really shrinks in the winter time," Giraffe observed more than once to his friend Peter o'Possum as they shared a bowl of hot broth around his fire. He did not see Princess Isabel or Isabel very often after the snow began to accumulate although their father had a fine sleigh: summoning Zane and Zack to pull it and rousing Oscar the footman to harness them was almost too much trouble; besides, Oscar always complained that harnessing zebras was no part of his job description. So the royal family stayed home during the winter like almost everyone else.

This was what made the Christmas party so important. It was an occasion of assembly and departure, a time of cheer and farewell, for all Montanans. And especially now that they had chosen the place for their celebration and the tree, they were determined to make the most of it.

❆ ❆ ❆

Putting lights on the tree was their first order of business. Kanga, with a little help from Balleau, had saved a great ball of beeswax, and she hoped the beavers would help her make lots of little candles, which the possums could fasten to all the twigs and branches.

"Candles on the tree, that's an old European custom," she explained, "and very cheery, isn't it, Roo?"

Peter o'Possum, however, didn't like the idea at all:

what if just one candle fell or dripped? His pine would catch on fire for sure.

"I want us to have a beautiful tree as much as anyone, but I couldn't enjoy Christmas if I was worrying all the time about my home burning down."

Giraffe, to whom he explained these feelings, understood them perfectly and suggested an alternative. "We are lucky to have all this wax," he said, "and grateful to you, Kanga, for donating it to us; candle light is lovely and seasonal: I'd hate to have a Christmas without it. But maybe Peter's tree is not the best or safest place for such a display—especially if it would make Peter uneasy."

"Roo and I would never think of endangering Peter's tree, would we, Roo?" Kanga said. "But we did go to some trouble collecting this wax; and the candles we hoped to make, when flame makes the scent of honey begin to rise, are very festive."

"That's true, Kanga," Giraffe agreed, "but what about making several large candles instead of so many tiny ones, and placing them all around the ground beneath Peter's tree to mark off our Christmas place? We could set big candles beside each path to guide all the folks of Montana to the celebration."

"The other beavers and I," added Bo Bo, who was present at this meeting, "would be happy to make candlestands out of the snow we sweep off the floor. They would extinguish any stray sparks."

"Oh, Giraffe," Kanga said, "that will be jolly; that will be jolly, won't it, Roo?"

Peter o'Possum seemed satisfied with Giraffe's suggestion, too, once it was explained to him. "Assuming," he said, "you direct the beavers, Bo Bo, to build big snow cups or plates to catch any sparks blown off those candles."

When Giraffe reported this plan down at the pond, however, he got a different response. "Lights make a tree, Giraffe, let me tell you," Hal the hippo said with conviction.

"Oh, yes," Allison cried, "we must have lights on our tree."

"I agree," said Casper as he finished biting off the tough head of a catfish; and giving his tail an emphatic twitch, he proclaimed, "what's a Christmas tree without lights?"

"In the Florida zoo," Allison recollected wistfully, "we reptiles had our own tree right in the center of the reptile house, and it was covered with lights: there were glass fireflies that glowed off and on, different varieties of glass fish with lights in their eyes, electric candles, balls that shone like leaded windows, and a glistening electric eel, which Mr. Masters the manager himself wrapped round and round the tree just before our attendants turned it on. (That's why I had trouble at first with the eel you served me for lunch the other day, Casper.) Our tree was so bright and festive—the best time of the year. And on Christmas morning every one of us was served his favorite meal—pompano, for me; I loved to take that delectable fish behind my old cypress log and feast."

"I get the idea," Giraffe replied when Allison paused for breath. "I'm afraid we won't be able to provide you with such pleasures, Allison, not this Christmas; but there is a plan to illuminate our own pine tree. I myself possess several kinds of electric bulbs, red and blue and green ones, and some, which I acquired in Billings last fall, that look just like candle flames, red and gold and white at the tips."

"But how will you make them light up, Giraffe?" asked Hal.

"Yes," said Casper, snapping his jaws in disgust, "electric lights are no good without electric power, and there's no use in your hoping I will catch an electric eel for you; our eels haven't been charged." And Casper laughed out loud, if you can imagine that.

But Allison and Hal were too concerned with the tree to join in. "Yes, Giraffe," Allison said, "how will you light your bulbs—and mine, too, for that matter, because I brought a couple of sparkling fireflies, a sweet glass pompano, and a miniature cypress log all the way from Florida?"

"Let me tell you," Hal assured his two friends after thinking for a minute, "Giraffe has already considered this, and I bet he has a plan."

"The king has an emergency generator, which he bought some years ago for the palace hospital," Giraffe announced, "and he has offered it to us. It will prove quite adequate to illuminate all the lights we have. Zane and Zack, wearing their Christmas antlers, are drawing it over to Peter's tree on the royal sledge even as we speak."

The effect of this news on his friends was everything Giraffe could have hoped for.

"A generator!" Casper exclaimed, "a generator! Well, Giraffe, you fooled us this time. I guess we'll have to save my eel for next Christmas."

"Oh, Giraffe," Allison chimed in, "with your lights and mine, won't the tree shine!"

"That's splendid, Giraffe," Hal agreed, "except for the wires. Electric lights all take wires, as our friend Rudolph might explain to us, and if the wires show, the effect of the lights is ruined. Wires dangling beneath branches or lights dangling so the wires supporting them show—it makes a Christmas tree look spidery, Giraffe, let me tell you, and spoils the whole display."

"Perhaps you should direct the stringing of the lights, Hal," Giraffe suggested, "and make sure the little possums who place them will hide all the wires."

"I'm not sure I'm the best person to be trusted with this task," Hal replied modestly.

"Of course you are, Hal," snapped Casper, and then he snapped his jaws together for emphasis. "You obviously have a better understanding of Christmas-tree lights than most people."

"We don't expect you to do much climbing," Giraffe explained.

"No," said Allison, who was beginning to understand her new friends, "not a whole lot of climbing."

"You can circle beneath the tree and direct things from below," Giraffe assured his friend. "You're very good at directing."

"Yes," Hal agreed with some satisfaction, "I am good at directing, let me tell you, and I do want the lights on our tree to look right. Very well, then, Giraffe, I will accept this responsibility."

"Most of our lights," Giraffe told the new director, "are stored at the palace along with our ornaments; Oscar the footman will show you where they are. I believe you should start right away, because we want all the lights in place before we begin to attach the other ornaments, don't you agree, Hal?"

"Yes," Hal acknowledged, "the lights must be fixed first of all." And he immediately climbed out of the pond to assume his duties. "It's quite a jaunt over to the palace," he said, "and although I'm actually very agile on land, I'd better get going."

The ornaments were just as important as the lights, and almost every citizen of the state had a favorite one or two which had to be well and properly placed. Kanga and Roo, for instance, owned a box of glass figures of Pooh and Piglet and Eeyore and Rabbit and Christopher Robin. The head had been broken off Christopher Robin a few years ago, but Kanga fastened it back with honey, and it looked pretty good. Hal had a copy of Mount Rainier he'd acquired on one of his yearly trips to the west coast, "Although," as Rudolph the raccoon assured their friends, "it hardly hints at the peak's true grandeur." And Gloria the gorilla had received a miniature felt bowler as a bonus in the package that brought her the present for Dr. Oscar the orangutan.

Giraffe bought a tiny pair of ruby slippers on his

trip to Billings with Isabel and Princess Isabel to see *The Wizard of Oz,* and the two girls had found a splendid glass giraffe. They hoped to put it on the top of the tree. There was also a sleigh full of toys, a crew of elves, a pear, a bear, a bird with a bristly tail, a little set of tea things, a number of musical instruments, a mustard jar that nobody could explain, a steaming mug of either mead or wassail created from amber by either Kanga or Catherine the cook, a few beautiful old medicine bottles to which Dr. Oscar the orangutan had fastened hooks when they became empty, a pretty pebble with a hole in it Marvin the mole had come across in his wanderings, an interesting shell Hal had found on the shore of the Pacific—a conch shell, as Rudolph the raccoon explained—an empty marmalade jar that seemed to have accompanied Kanga from England, and the bandage—plated in bronze—which Dr. Oscar had wrapped around the broken tail of Billy the beaver. This collection belonged to all Montanans, and everybody added to it.

The beavers were busy this year chewing pretty ornaments out of the different woods of their state. They made a royal king and queen from royal spruce, a pineapple from pine, an acorn from oak, a spray of holly from a branch of holly, and a fine pair of reptiles, a crocodile and an alligator, from birch bark. The crocodile Bo Bo painted a shiny chocolate, but the alligator he left as it was, a silvery white. Ella wanted to offer the beavers the tips of her tusks for carvings of Isabel and Princess Isabel, but Giraffe convinced her ivory would be too hard for their teeth. Actually, he realized she would need her tusks, tips and all, to get through the winter. Instead, she gouged up two pieces of ice from her little stream at his suggestion and shaped these, with some help from Rudolph the raccoon, who was very dextrous, into sparkling figures of the two royal sisters, Isabel dressed like Florence Nightingale in a nurse's costume and Princess Isabel distinguished by the tiara and the cloak she had recently worn to the meeting.

Hal assembled the lights, stopping by the patio to fetch Allison's little collection and then at the cave to get Giraffe's. He carried these, safely wrapped in a canvas bag, over to the palace where, with the help of Isabel, who was recovering from the flu, and Oscar the footman, he got all the rest. It made quite a load and a fragile load to boot, but luckily Hal was very agile—as he was happy to remind his friends—and, by packing all the lights in green slime, he was able to transport every one safely to the base of Peter o'Possum's pine. The generator was already in place behind a holly bush; Rudolph had checked it and attached the wires. So once Hal had organized the little possums—not a perfectly easy task—he began to arrange the lights.

Oscar the footman got out the old ornaments at the same time he retrieved the lights, and Marian the maid dusted them, so they were ready when Giraffe, who always took charge of gathering and placing the ornaments, came over to pick them up. Marian broke one, a glass blackbird, but only one, and there were several other birds, a cardinal, an indigo bunting, a Baltimore oriole (the one with the bristly tail) and a scarlet tanager, so Giraffe found plenty of winged ornaments for the top of the tree. Besides, new ornaments were arriving at the base of Peter o'Possum's pine from all over Montana. Leo the lion, at Lucy's urging, donated the scarlet bow he had once worn in his tail; Billy the beaver brought a piece of coal shaped like Florida from the Montana train; Zane and Zack donated their antlers—no small gift; and the king sent over a ball made from tattered twenties the queen had stuck together with honey—or so it seemed to Giraffe when he tried to fasten it to the tree. Catherine the cook sent a string of popcorn—very pretty; Casper created a sort of mobile from fish spines; and Marian the maid contributed a colorful rope of old socks. These were draped around the tree as festoons, along with Giraffe's green sash, once all the other ornaments were in place.

But first came the lights.

"No, no, Percy," Hal cried out, raising his voice, not for the first time, to the friskiest and most mischievous of the possums, four of whom, at his direction, were attaching the lights to their tree. "You must not put your weight on the wires."

Percy, who had just hung Allison the alligator's cypress log on a small branch near the outer edge of the tree, was trying it out as a swing; and it made a pretty good swing, too.

"I wish Giraffe were here," Hal muttered to himself. "He'd know how to keep these rascals in line."

Just then, Hal's wish was fulfilled. "Hello, Percy," Giraffe called out as he sauntered into view. "That looks like a great ride."

"It is, Giraffe," Percy replied as he steadied himself by grabbing one of the wires with his tail. "Why don't you come up and give it a try? I would invite Hal, but he's too serious for this kind of fun."

As he swung away, his siblings, Pam and Polly and Phil, all of whom had paused to greet Giraffe, broke into gales of laughter, not exactly Christmas laughter. Giraffe might have joined in, but he saw Hal was anxious and unhappy, so he kept a straight face and urged Percy to be more careful of Allison's log. "She brought it all the way from Florida," he explained. "It has a serious sentimental value for her; and it would surely break, Percy, if you shook it loose. So would you," he added as he saw that Percy was losing his grip on the wire. In fact, Giraffe rushed right over and, stretching his neck up into the tree, grabbed Percy with his tongue just as the little fellow started to fall.

This restored an air of purpose and duty, to which even Percy responded. When Hal called to Pam to tighten a leaded ball or asked Phil to make sure one of the electric candles was pointing up and not down—"The way real candles point," Hal insisted—the little Possums followed his directions without a smirk. Giraffe's presence helped: he could reach up and correct many of the problems posed by the wires; and his serious concentration on these and on the wiring problems above him, which the little possums had to fix, kept everybody happily employed. Percy made the last adjustment, wrapping a candle tighter around a branch up near the top of the tree and hiding the last sign of electricity—or almost the last sign. Nothing is perfect. But Hal was satisfied at last.

"I believe it's done," he said with a sigh, glad to give up the responsibilities of direction. "What do you think, Giraffe?"

"I think we must invite Allison over, if you would be willing to fetch her, Hal, and click on the generator; then we'll be able to make sure we've illuminated our tree."

"Oh, Hal," Allison said, when the lights first came on, "aren't they lovely! Look at my cypress log," she exclaimed, as she inspected it more closely—suppressing a little lump in her throat—"and all the candles: they all point up, just like they should; so many different colors; and there's my sweet pompano, swimming among the green branches. It's beautiful, isn't it, Giraffe? Hal and the little possums have put every light in just the right place!"

❄ ❄ ❄

Next came the hanging of the ornaments, most of which were, as Giraffe warned the crew of possums and coons their fathers had assembled, even more fragile than the lights. He told them how Marian the maid had broken the blackbird and showed them Christopher Robin's patched head and begged them to be careful. And, with a little supervision from Peter and Rudolph, they were.

Giraffe's plan was to begin at the top of the tree, attaching the birds and several of the smaller ornaments there, and then to work down, fixing the ornaments representing his friends low enough so everybody could enjoy them. Princess Isabel and Isabel, who had just joined the ornament crew, urged him to direct Percy, the nimblest and bravest of the possums, to station their Giraffe at the tip top of the tree, and Giraffe had a little trouble persuading them to give up this idea.

"I'm very grateful you wish to do me such an honor," he said, "and the ornament itself is as beautiful as a giraffe could be, but I would feel very conspicuous up there on top—and a little dizzy as well: we giraffes like to keep our feet on the ground."

"I suppose you'd prefer to put Hal the hippo up there," Princess Isabel replied.

"Or," said Isabel, somewhat more reasonably, "this carving of Peter o'Possum."

"I'd much prefer to see one of the two ice princesses up there," Giraffe replied with a good humor nothing could quench, "except that each of them will appear to such good effect surrounded by a canopy of foliage."

"I think my Mt. Rainier would look best up there," said Hal, who had lingered on after the lights were in place.

"Not a bad idea," Rudolph acknowledged, trying to practice a little of Giraffe's tact. "A peak at the peak of our tree. But it seems to me," he continued, "the very best image for such an eminent spot is the one that revealed our tree to us, the image of Rudolf the red-nosed reindeer. I'll never forget how he appeared above us when we seemed to have reached an impasse in our deliberations and then how he spiraled round and round this, the perfect tree: you remember, don't you, Princess Isabel?"

"Yes," she admitted, "that was a great moment for all Montanans."

Luckily, Bo Bo the beaver, a very clever artist, had just carved and painted a Rudolf and tricked it out in harness and bells, ready to take off on its Christmas trip. So with general agreement, the nimble Percy was directed to place Rudolf the red-nosed reindeer at the tip top of Peter o'Possum's pine.

The next steps went smoothly. The little possums decorated the highest branches, attaching the birds and a number of tiny silver stars. The little coons scrambled up to the next highest, after some encouragement from their father and Giraffe. They hung up Santa and his elves along with fruits, tea things, musical instruments, crowns, jars and all of Kanga's distant friends. Giraffe himself, stretching to his full height, placed most of the new ornaments and, somewhat lower where everybody could view them, the different citizens of the state. In that level of the tree, the king and queen, recently carved by the beavers, held their court, closely attended by their sparkling daughters and all their servants, Oscar the footman, Catherine the cook, Marian the maid (wearing a bandaid across her face), and Fergus the footman's son. Giraffe stood at the king's right hand, as Isabel and Princess Isabel insisted, and all the others were beautifully grouped around below. Near the zebras, who stood together front to back, Giraffe placed Ella the elephant, complete with tusks, bearing a little possum on her back.

Lowest on the tree were the special things. Each citizen of the state was allowed to place one ornament on this level. Fergus the footman's son attached his Harvard letter here; Gloria hung her tiny felt bowler, a choice only she and Giraffe could understand; near by, Dr. Oscar the orangutan hung a blown-glass banana; and Allison, with some help from Giraffe, draped a velveteen eel. Rudolph the raccoon attached a model of an octagonal pavilion he had created from splinters; the zebras hung their antlers; and Giraffe, the ruby slippers.

The king attached a tiny bowl and the queen, the blackbird, which she had mended herself. Casper, at Allison's insistence, dangled his olympic gold; Leo affixed Lucy's olympic bronze; and Balleau the bear stuck on something made from honey that Giraffe interpreted as a sculpture of his friend Kanga. Kanga herself hung a tiny mug with Peter o'Possum's initials scratched on it. And Peter arranged the images of his little ones the beavers had carved for him, hanging each one of the four from his own prehensile wire.

Finally came the assemblage and the distribution of the presents, all or most of which were wrapped in shiny foil. The king, a merry old soul now he had completed this year's counting, furnished every citizen a roll of glossy paper that bore a map of Montana; and many of the presents including Giraffe's gifts to Isabel, Princess Isabel, Zane and Zack—all four gifts wrapped separately—appeared in this patriotic attire. But everybody had personal paper, too: Billy's showed his locomotive, Casper's, the car Billy had modified for Allison, Zane and Zack's, a pattern of burdock leaves, Dr. Oscar's, a medical kit, Allison's, a likeness of Mr. Masters the manager stamping from foot to foot (which everyone mistook for Gloria). Rudolph's showed a picture of Hal and so did Hal's.

Presents wrapped in such paper accumulated as if by magic all through Christmas eve day until the trunk of Peter o'Possum's pine was completely hidden. There were a couple of big presents—one addressed to Ella, for example, in a great cylindrical box—that made all the folks wonder. And one for Allison the alligator, which smelled suspiciously like the ocean. But everybody, even the little ones, tried to keep their notions to themselves. And nobody thought to touch or shake even the most exciting or mysterious of the gifts.

Just at dusk, Bo Bo clicked on the lights and lit the candles, ending with the big ones that marked the entrances to the celebration. Then there was a pause so the king and his entourage could make the first appearance.

Soon the royal sleigh arrived, drawn over from the palace by Zane and Zack. It carried the king and queen, Isabel and Princess Isabel, their presents, and, tied on the back, a large thermos, a vat really, full of the royal wassail. The king, who furnished his subjects all their Christmas cheer, prided himself on his wassail—a fact Giraffe brought to the notice of his fellow citizens. Immediately behind the royal sleigh came the royal sledge drawn this year by Balleau the bear and Fergus the footman's son.

"I don't know, Giraffe, I really don't know," the king said when he met his old friend, who always arrived for Christmas as early as possible: "When I asked Ella the elephant to help with the sledge, she declined. She told me some story, Giraffe, some mother-goose tale, about a strained tusk. That's not like her, is it? Ella is usually so helpful. If Balleau the bear had not just happened to pass by the palace on his way here, I don't know what we would have done. Fergus the footman's son is a stout lad—he wrestled for Harvard, you know—but he couldn't have pulled the sledge by himself, certainly not with his dad and Catherine the cook and Marian the maid riding in it, not to speak, Giraffe, of the second vat of my wassail and this great black bundle of ours."

"Your majesty was very lucky—and so were we all— Balleau just happened by," Giraffe responded and gave Balleau a grateful smile. "I'm glad you were able to load the bundle. Perhaps Balleau could help me put it here a little behind the other gifts before Ella shows up?"

"I'll be glad to, Giraffe," Balleau said: "it's a big dude. For Ella, eh? I wonder what it could be."

"Wait and see, Balleau, like everyone else," said the king with a chuckle, "wait and see."

Allison the alligator and Casper the crocodile arrived next, then Hal the hippo, puffing a little, and gradually all the other inhabitants of Montana. The possums just dropped from their home, of course, but everyone else, except Dr. Oscar the orangutan, who came swinging through the trees, waddled or trudged or trotted or slunk or scrambled or hopped through one or another of the candlelit gateways into their Christmas place.

"Oh, Roo," exclaimed Kanga, when she caught her breath, "look at all our candles: aren't they festive?"

"I especially approve of the placing of Rudolf the red-nosed reindeer," said Leo as he ran his eyes up the tree, "that's exactly as I would have commanded."

"And the lighted candle just below it," Lucy added, "is just perfect."

"My favorites are the antlers," the queen said.

"Yes, yes," the king agreed, "but look at our court."

Leo, who turned his eye where the king had suggested, was about to question the placing of Giraffe when Princess Isabel cried out: "There's Giraffe: doesn't he look wonderful, standing beside daddy?"

"Yes," Isabel agreed, "daddy's lucky to have such a counselor."

"I believe, your majesty," Giraffe broke in, "that Hal and his assistants have lighted the tree better than I ever saw it lighted before."

"Yes," said the king, "the tree is beautiful, beautiful."

The crowd had gathered quickly except for Rudolph the raccoon and Ella the elephant. While those who were present waited and fretted—because nobody except the little ones could think of opening the celebration until everyone had arrived—they speculated.

"I don't know what to think about Ella," the king said. "Maybe she really does have a strained tusk."

"A strained tusk?" exclaimed the queen.

"I hope she shows up," muttered Gloria. "I worked all fall on her trunk muffler."

"Should someone go into the meadow and check on her?" asked Kanga.

"I'll go, if you should like me to, your majesty," said either Zane or Zack.

"No, no," cried Rudolph as he came bustling up the path from the direction of the pond. "I've just left her a little way behind me. She had gotten lost, she said, in the dusk. I straightened her out, and I've run on ahead so you wouldn't worry."

Rudolph did seem a little out of breath. And he'd forgotten the red-and-white striped stocking cap he always sported on such occasions as this. When Leo the lion asked him about it, Rudolph seemed a little flustered—and that wasn't like him. But before he could explain, Ella the elephant burst into the Christmas clearing.

She looked even more breathless and distracted than Rudolph.

"Where's your wreath, Ella?" Kanga asked with some concern. "It's Christmas."

Before Ella could respond, the king, who'd been examining her, inquired, "Is that green slime on your trunk?"

"Green slime?" Hal exclaimed.

"You didn't get so lost," the queen asked, "you fell in the pond, did you? That sounds like something my maid,

Marian, might do."

"No, your majesty," Ella replied, "my eyesight is bad, particularly at dusk, but not that bad."

Everybody was looking at Ella now, and Peter o'Possum pointed out a big black smudge on her hip. "It sure looks like soot."

"Soot," said Billy the beaver skeptically. "I don't think so. I stopped the train just outside the station this evening, and I'd surely have seen Ella if she had been wandering around."

"Why did you stop outside the station, Billy?" asked the king.

"Well, your majesty, well," Billy replied, "I was afraid I'd get in ahead of time."

"Ahead of time?" Leo the lion growled, "you're always an hour late, like the time you were bringing Allison and Giraffe home from the Florida Zoo."

"Well," said Billy with a little grin, "an hour late is on time for the Montana Line."

"Lame, lame," Leo roared with disgust.

"Yes, yes," said the king, "but now we are all here, anyway. And so it is time," he continued in a formal tone, "to begin our celebration." He climbed onto the dais, which the beavers had built under Peter o'Possum's tree for this occasion, and proclaimed: "The Montana Christmas celebration is now officially in session."

"We will begin with wassail and music," the king announced. "My fiddlers three, transported here by train from the Tennessee hills, were a little late in arriving, as you have heard, but not too late. I call them now!"

As he spoke, sure enough, everybody could hear the fiddlers playing away as they came up the path that led from the station: they rendered "Deck the Hall," "The Boar's Head," "Greensleeves," and "The Tennessee Waltz" as they entered the Christmas clearing. And then, after much applause, while Oscar the footman, Catherine the cook, Fergus the footman's son, and Marian the maid served everyone a brimming cup of wassail, they played "Rudolf the Red-nosed Reindeer," "Joy to the World," and "Santa Claus is Coming to Town."

Oscar handed a special thimble to Roo, another to Marvin the mole, and a nice bucket to Ella for their convenience; and Ella, who seemed to have recovered, generously squirted wassail down the throats of Casper and Allison. Everybody requested seconds, and while they were being served, the fiddlers played "Hail, Montana," "Good King Wenceslaus," and "Winter Wonderland."

"Isn't this wassail good?" Kanga exclaimed to Peter o'Possum.

"Yes, " he replied loudly, "almost as good as your mead"—a comment the king wasn't perfectly sure about.

"I believe," cried Giraffe, "it's even better than it was last year: my compliments to the palace staff."

"It's delicious, let me tell you," sputtered Hal, who was sucking up his wassail through a straw.

"Yes," added Dr. Oscar the orangutan, "it's as good, I believe, as Gloria's tasty banana punch"—a belief Gloria would question him about as the winter advanced.

The king, who found these compliments exhilarating, called for another bowlful and then announced from the dais, where he was sitting with the queen, "It's time for the presents: Isabel and Princess Isabel have graciously agreed to preside over this part of our celebration. But first, perhaps, another round of wassail for everyone and a little more music. What about 'Bring a Torch Jeanette Isabella'—Isabella, I've always loved that name—and 'Good King Wenceslaus' again. What do you say, fiddlers?"

During the interlude of music and toasting that followed this command, Leo the lion proposed "Rudolf the red-nosed reindeer!"

"Hear, hear!" shouted Rudolph the Raccoon.

"Hal, the creator of the lights," whinnied Zane and Zack, "and Giraffe, the master of the ornaments!"

"I want to toast Bo Bo," Kanga interjected, "for placing the candles."

"True, true," agreed Giraffe, who recognized the toasting might get out of hand and brought it to a satisfactory conclusion by raising his voice: "I give you our king, King Cole, the founder of our celebration!"

Then, after everyone had toasted the king, the royal siblings stepped forward and started distributing the gifts. Princess Isabel went first: "Here's one for Giraffe, beautifully wrapped in the royal Montana paper. Open it, Giraffe, and let us all see."

It was a warm winter coverall, perfectly tailored to fit Giraffe from head to foot; it had galoshes attached and was colored exactly like Giraffe himself, yellow with brown spots, so he would look the same with it on or off.

"Now," said Princess Isabel, "you don't have any excuse, Giraffe, for not visiting me during the winter, do you?"

"No," Giraffe replied, "if I can manage to get this collar over my head."

"I'll help you, Giraffe," said Peter o'Possum, "if you'll let me ride on your back to the palace sometimes."

"It's a deal, Peter," Giraffe responded.

"Here are two packages," said Isabel in turn, "that seem to be almost identical—for Zane and Zack the zebras. Let's see: this one is labeled 'for the zebra with white stripes over both eyes,' and this one 'for the zebra with a black stripe over one of his eyes.'" Isabel looked very closely at the two friends to make sure of giving the correct gift to each one.

"Look," each of them cried out at the same time, "a name plate: a beautiful gold disk inlaid with my name in black onyx."

"Zane," said Zane, and "Zack," said Zack, both at the same time; "Mine is set in a velvet case and attached to a velvet necklace."

Isabel helped each zebra put on his own name plate and stepped back to admire them. "Very grand," she assured them, "and I can read them from several feet away. I hope you never remove them."

"I won't," said Zane and Zack together, and they

faced one another so that each of them could admire the other's present.

"Here's something for you, Mother," announced Princess Isabel, "a jar— 'to aid the queen in her duties'—it says; and here's some writing wrapped around it."

"Oh, your majesty," Kanga cried out before the queen could respond, "Roo and I hope you like it, don't we, Roo?"

"It's mead, your majesty," Peter o'Possum explained as the queen was examining the contents of her jar, "made from honey: it's really delicious. Please try it."

"Yes, my dear, take a little snort," the king suggested, "take a little snort and tell us what you think."

"Very well," sniffed the queen suspiciously, "for your sake, my dear." After a sip, which everyone watched anxiously, the queen smiled with approval: "Quite acceptable, yes, quite acceptable."

Everyone heaved a little sigh of relief, and then Kanga spoke up again: "If your majesty really enjoys our drink, mine's and Roo's, there is our recipe, wrapped around the jar. Perhaps Catherine the cook could brew you up a batch."

"Yes, perhaps," responded the queen graciously, and to show her sincerity, she tipped up her jar and took a healthy swallow.

"And here is a little box for Hal the hippo," reported Isabel: "It says, 'so you'll always know where you are.'"

"What is it," said Hal with some anxiety, "a watch? Does it tick? I don't really have the right wrist for a watch, let me tell you."

"Open it, silly," Princess Isabel commanded, "and find out."

"Yes," urged Rudolph the raccoon with impatience, "open it, Hal."

"It's a—it's a—it's a . . ," mumbled Hal, as he tore at the paper.

"Here, Hal, my clumsy friend," said Rudolph, who was almost unable to contain himself: "let me help."

"It's a—it's a compass, a compass," Hal announced to everyone, "a compass with a strong brass chain: just what I needed, let me tell you," and he put the chain around his neck. "It fits perfectly," he said with excitement: "Now I can take the short cut on my journey to Oregon."

"It's very becoming, Hal," said Zane and Zack, as they examined Hal's compass, "but look at our name plates."

"Comparisons later," the king commanded, "let's get on with these gifts: we've got a long way to go. And, by the way, Marian, could I have another bowl of our tasty wassail? I believe it's even better than last year's. Won't you join me in another wee drop, my dear?" he asked the queen.

"No, thank you, my dear," the queen replied with a smile, "I think I'll stay with this delicious mead. Let Marian fill your bowl again."

"Speaking of Marian," said Princess Isabel, "here's a little present with her name on it."

It was a very small present indeed, just big enough for Dr. Oscar the orangutan, who stepped forward as if on call, to hold in the palm of his hand. He'd just received and donned his present, a handsome black bowler, so everyone recognized him immediately, as Gloria had hoped.

"Let me help you with this, Marian," he suggested in a very professional manner as he held out for her inspection an elegant nose.

He already had his facial glue ready, a secret formula of banana oil, honey and pine gum; and almost before Marian the maid knew what he was about, Dr. Oscar had snatched the bandaid she'd been wearing on the front of her face and applied her new nose. Then he handed her the little mirror which accompanied this present and invited her to judge the result. Bo Bo the beaver, who designed, carved, and tinted this gift, had got the proportions and the color just right, and the face Marian beheld in the mirror was even prettier than the one she thought the blackbird had ruined. Or so it struck Fergus the footman's son, who'd never given Marian a second glance before. Although she was not the fairest in the land, Marian looked remarkably pretty, especially now as she blushed with pleasure and pride at her reflection.

"Good, good," said the king, "now, girl, how about that wassail?"

From this point on, the presents flowed thick and fast—and so of course did the wassail. Billy the beaver got a new railroad cap, which he had needed for some time; Bo Bo received a fine personalized dust pan; Leo and Lucy the lions got matching ribbons—"They glow in the dark," Isabel assured them; Marvin the mole was fitted with a pair of thick, tinted glasses—for those times he felt like joining his friends on the surface; and for Rudolph the raccoon there was a picture of Henry Clay's home bound with a red-and-white striped scarf, a match for the stocking hat he had forgotten to wear to the party.

Gloria, who had received a selection of pills for dyspepsia—not a very appropriate gift for Christmas—gave Ella the elephant a trunk muffler. After all, she explained to Giraffe, she had spent all fall weaving it. And Kanga got a woolen pouch lining, which, at Peter o'Possum's insistence, Patsy o'Possum had modeled for her.

"It's lined with silk and fastened with a smooth plastic zipper," Peter told Kanga.

"Oh, look, Roo," Kanga said, once she got used to it, "now we can go out no matter how cold it is, and you'll be as snug as if you were home in bed."

Isabel presented Oscar the footman an electric razor, depriving him of a favorite excuse; and Princess Isabel handed Fergus the footman's son a fancy toilet kit complete with aftershave and deodorant, which he realized he'd be making good use of.

The king's family gave the king, "who had everything," an Arabian hookah with a long flexible stem, in the hope that he might enjoy the fine aromatic tobacco Giraffe had brought him from Kentucky without inhaling.

"I really called for a pipe," he muttered to Oscar the footman, who was refilling his bowl. "But I'll try to get used to smoking this hookah," he said aloud to the queen, who was taking another wee drop from her Christmas jar.

This expression of gratitude, somewhat to her daughters' surprise, the queen seemed to find acceptable. She was in a much better mood, luckily, than she had been at the beginning of the celebration.

Princess Isabel smiled a little ruefully when she opened the gift of fine plaid gloves, which would help her, as Giraffe suggested, to assist her father in his chilly counting house.

But Isabel laughed happily when she received the silk t-shirt Giraffe had acquired for her at a shop in the Florida Zoo. "I love the picture on the front of Mr. Masters the manager squatting and smoking a hookah," she exclaimed.

The queen immediately brought this picture to the king's attention: "If Mr. Masters can enjoy a hookah, my dear, surely you can."

Then at last came the presents everybody had been anticipating, the box from the sea, as Princess Isabel called it when presenting it to Allison the alligator, and the large hollow cylinder.

The cylinder, which was addressed to "Ella the elephant, at the start of a hard winter," people had guessed to be a drum, an urn, a rug, and even a cheese, although the Swiss, as Rudolph insisted, never made a cheese with so big a hole.

"It's tin...it's paper...it's plastic," different people exclaimed as Ella gradually unwrapped it with her tusks and her trunk.

"Don't step on it, Ella," Giraffe warned her.

"What is it? What is it?" Ella asked, even when she got it completely opened.

"Why," announced Billy the beaver after a few moments of inspection, "it's a silo, a do-it-yourself silo."

"You'll have a lot of fun putting that together," said Casper the crocodile, snapping his jaws: "If I weren't about to be frozen solid, I'd give you a helping claw. It looks like you'll need it."

"I'm sure Billy and Rudolph, both of whom are dextrous," Giraffe said with an assurance he saw that Ella needed, "will be happy to help assemble it before the winter closes in."

"Of course we will, Ella, of course we will help you assemble it," they both agreed.

"Thank you," Ella responded, but she still seemed to be a little bemused: it had been a very demanding holiday. "What will I do with it after it is assembled, Giraffe? An empty silo?"

"Of course," she answered herself somewhat dubiously, "I can fill it in the summertime for next winter, if I get through this one."

"Well," said the king, coming out of a little snooze, "what do you say to a nice load of hay?" And as he spoke, Balleau the bear pulled out the great bundle that had come on the king's sledge, and shouted, "Merry Christmas!"

"Oh, Giraffe," Ella exclaimed, "oh, Balleau, oh, your majesty! What can I say? This will be the best winter I ever had in Montana."

The fresh-frozen pompano, which Casper had asked Billy the beaver to bring to Montana for Allison the alligator, seemed a little anti-climactic after the Christmas Giraffe and the king and Balleau had presented to Ella, but it didn't strike Allison that way.

"It's just like the pompano I used to get for Christmas in the zoo," Allison said excitedly as she opened the box and scraped away the packing ice. "Just like the one I used to eat all alone behind my old cypress log. Even nicer, Casper." And tears gathered in her eyes.

"She's remembering her old cypress log, let me tell you," Hal murmured, explaining the situation to those who had gathered around. "She's been homesick for it all autumn."

"I'm sorry, Casper, everybody," Allison apologized: "I'm just being silly." And then, trying to give a little smile— a hard thing for an alligator—she spoke directly to Casper, whose sympathy had almost overcome him: "I hope that you will share this delicious fish with me at a little farewell party in our humble abode."

"A little farewell party?" Casper echoed, clamping his jaws together as he spoke.

"I mean," Allison replied, only partly understanding his feelings, "a party for you and me to say farewell to all our friends before we settle down in our little mud home for the winter."

"Oh," said Casper, snapping his jaws in relief, "oh, yes: won't everyone join Allison and me at our humble abode for a farewell party? We are both beginning to stiffen up for winter, and we're anxious to say farewell to all our friends, farewell, that is, until spring."

❄ ❄ ❄

The little ones were nestled all snug in their beds, hoping Santa would come and fill their stockings before they woke; and most of the royal party, the king, the queen, and Isabel, who was not quite over the flu, were ready for their long winter's nap; but all the rest of the revelers, including Princess Isabel, were happy to accept the invitation of Allison the alligator and Casper the crocodile.

Before they all left for the pond, however, the king requested his hookah and his bowl—"Just one more drop," he said—and called his three fiddlers to perform "Goodnight, Irene," "'Til We Meet Again," and "Auld Lang Syne."

"Everybody join in," the king commanded when the fiddlers began the last of these songs: "Everybody join in," he ordered. And everybody did.

Then, as Bo Bo clicked off the Christmas tree lights and began to blow out the candles, the royal party was bundled into the royal sleigh. Oscar the footman harnessed up Zane and Zack, both proudly wearing their name plates; and the sleigh, followed by the fiddlers, still playing "Auld Lang Syne," slowly made its way back to the palace. Kanga and Roo had also been invited to wedge in. The queen, who had become quite jolly, graciously offered to drop them off on the way. The rest, as they turned toward the pond, heard the soulful strains of "Auld Lang Syne," although it finally blended with the sound of the wind, echo and re-echo through the forest.

Ella the elephant, holding one of the big candles in her trunk, led the procession to the pond. Astride her back, she was carrying Princess Isabel, whom she had promised the queen to bring home when all the farewells were said. The beavers had fixed two candles each on the backs of Allison and Casper, having been assured by Rudolph the raccoon and the reptiles themselves that hot wax wouldn't burn their scaly skin. Allison and Casper followed Ella the elephant, partly to provide light and partly to keep the parade from leaving them behind. Gloria the gorilla, Leo and Lucy the lions, Peter o'Possum (who carried Marvin the mole), Rudolph the raccoon, the beavers Billy and Bo Bo, Balleau the bear (who was yawning mightily), and Hal the hippo trudged along after them in a casual single file; Dr. Oscar the orangutan swung along overhead. And Giraffe, who had to prod Hal and Balleau every now and then, brought up the rear.

When she reached the bank of the pond, Ella paused, flourished her candle, set it down, and trumpeted. And the others gradually gathered around.

As Allison scrambled around Ella, she took a survey of the whole pond: the patio—as Casper called it, the mud bank, which was their winter home, the beach, on which she and Casper and Giraffe and Hal had enjoyed their first picnic together, and the overflow that led to the residences of other friends, the raccoons and the beavers, and finally ran, as Rudolph the raccoon had informed her, to the Pacific Ocean.

She was thinking how much she had come to love this spot and waiting eagerly for Casper to join her when something about the patio caught her eye.

"What's that?" she asked Casper, who had just scrambled up beside her.

"What's what?" he responded, working his jaws.

"That shadow," Allison replied, "that dark shape at the back of the patio."

"What shape?" asked Casper, still gaping from the exertion of their hike.

"That shape, Casper, that big flat shadow behind our patio. You see it, don't you, Ella?"

"Yes," Ella admitted, "it might be Balleau if he weren't with us. Hello, Balleau," she said to the bear, who had just joined the circle.

"No, no," Allison exclaimed, "it isn't anything like you, Balleau."

"Look, Giraffe," she said, as the whole group assembled in the candle light, "you see what I'm looking at, don't you? It looks almost like a log, a big old log."

"A log?" said Giraffe.

"A log?" said Ella.

"A log?" said Rudolph, studying the patio closely.

"Yes," said Allison, "a log. Oh, my! oh, my!" she suddenly cried: "It's my old cypress log, oh, Casper, it is! It is! My old cypress log.

"Oh, Giraffe, oh, Ella, oh, Rudolph," Allison exclaimed as she swung toward each of them in turn. "That's how you got the slime on your tusk; that's why you forgot your cap; that's how you got the soot on your hip. Oh, Billy, that's why you stopped the train before you had reached the station. And, Balleau, that's why you just happened by the palace. A strained tusk, indeed: the queen was right. Oh, Ella, I hope you didn't really strain it putting my big old log in place."

"Merry Christmas, Allison," said Giraffe, "and welcome to Montana."

"Merry Christmas, merry Christmas," everybody shouted. And for a moment, "Merry Christmas" echoed through the woods of Montana.

Then they all sang "Auld Lang Syne" again.

And after that, they went their separate ways. Ella took Princess Isabel to the palace; Balleau slunk off to his den; Hal, accompanied a little way by Rudolph and the beavers, headed, with a backpack of·slime and his new compass, downstream to Oregon. The others just seemed to disappear into the winter darkness.

"I suppose that Casper and I will have to wait until spring to bask together beside my old cypress log," Allison said with a sigh to Giraffe, the last of the revelers to leave.

"Yes," Giraffe replied. "Ella can start enjoying her gifts right away; but spring will come."

Oh, yes," Allison exclaimed, "I can hardly wait."

www.GiraffeofMontana.com

Is it time for a game?

After reading each story, look at the picture again. Do you see a difference between what the writer wrote and the illustrator drew?

There's one difference in each picture.

For the answers and other games, go to:

www.GiraffeofMontana.com